Elle Woods

Blonde at Heart

Elle Woods

Blonde at Heart

Based on the character
created by Amanda Brown

Story by Natalie Standiford

HYPERION PAPERBACKS FOR CHILDREN
New York

First Edition

1 3 5 7 9 10 8 6 4 2

Printed in the United States of America
Library of Congress Cataloging-in-Publication Data on file

ISBN 0-7868-3843-4

Elle Woods

Blonde at Heart

Chapter 1

"YOU'RE NOT wearing *that*, are you?"

Elle's mother blocked the front door.

Elle was running late for school. She glanced down at her baggy clothes. "What's wrong with what I'm wearing?" she asked, though she knew the answer. Her oversized brown sweater was not Eva Woods's idea of Beverly Hills chic. But Elle didn't care. She loved big clothes, and she wanted to be comfortable.

"Elle looks adorable, as always," her father, Dr. Wyatt Woods, said. "She's my little big pussycat." He gave his daughter a squeeze.

Eva, dressed impeccably in a lavender Valentino suit, sighed. "What am I going to do with you?" she said to Elle. "I'm the only woman in California whose beautiful daughter doesn't care what she looks like. You redecorate your room every other week, but you won't wear anything but baggy pants and pink sneakers."

"Mom, I'm late. Are you going to let me out or not?"

"Oh, all right." Eva moved aside so Elle could leave. "But this weekend we're going shopping. And not at some chain store."

Elle Woods *was* a little different from her parents and their fancy Beverly Hills circle of friends. Her father was a prominent plastic surgeon in a town where face-lifts were considered a necessity, not a luxury. His blonde, glamorous wife was his best advertisement. His daughter, on the other hand, was "going through a phase."

"I'm no shrink," Wyatt said, and Elle thought, *That's for sure.* Her father was the type who thought a brisk round of tennis, followed by a dry martini, could cure any problem. "But I say our little girl is just that—a little girl. She'll grow up when she's good and ready."

"A late bloomer," Eva said. "Oh, well. It's probably good in the long run."

Elle was petite and pretty, with a heart-shaped

face and big blue eyes. But somehow people tended to notice her braces and her glasses first. Her hair—long, straight, no-color hair—was what some people might call mousy. It wasn't quite brown and it wasn't quite blonde, but an unremarkable shade in between.

When she was young and her mother dressed her, Elle was a baby beauty queen. By eight or nine, she was tired of sleeping with rollers in her hair and having to keep her lacy dresses nice. Eva kept buying fancy outfits for her, and Elle enjoyed arranging them by color in her closet. But somehow she never got around to actually wearing them.

"How do you expect boys to notice you when you dress in those baggy clothes?" her mother would ask.

Elle didn't care. Why would she want boys to notice her?

Sidney Ugman, the boy next door, had had a crush on her since kindergarten, and that was nothing but a pain. Sidney's attentions somehow always ended in disaster. Like the time he snorted milk up his nose and sprayed it all over her in the lunchroom, or the time in second grade when he tried to kiss her in the playground, yanking her off the monkey bars and knocking out one of her front teeth. Luckily it was a baby tooth and it was loose anyway, but still. Besides, he smelled like bologna, and Elle hated bologna. As far as she was concerned, being noticed by a boy brought nothing but trouble.

"I've got something for you." Elle found her best friend, Laurette Smythe, waiting for her on the front steps of Beverly Hills High School in a vintage housedress and clunky black boots. They'd been best friends since eighth grade, and were so inseparable people called them "Elle and L."

Elle reached into her backpack and pulled out a small box.

"Elle, you give me too many presents," Laurette said. She opened the box. Inside was a barrette shaped like the initial *L*, covered in red rhinestones.

"For while your hair's growing out," Elle said. "To help you through the awkward patches."

"It's beautiful." Laurette clipped back a chunk of her brown bangs with the barrette. "Thanks, Elle. You make the prettiest stuff."

They started into the school building, where they immediately ran into Francesca Morton.

"Elle and L!" Francesca said. "You know, I love that, the way your names go together! If only my name wasn't so sophisticated. Then I could have a cute little nickname, too."

"Good morning, Chessie," Elle said.

"Elle, remember what I told you?"

"Sorry," Elle said. "I just can't get used to it." Francesca had been called Chessie her whole life, but she'd suddenly decided, three days ago, that Chessie was too childish. She had ordered everyone to start calling her by her full name immediately. It wasn't catching on.

"I forgive you, Elle," Chessie said. "I know you space out sometimes." She looked Elle up and down. "Your style is so original. A baggy brown sweater. It looks just like something my grandfather wears."

"Thanks," Elle said, suddenly overcome by the familiar uncomfortable feeling Chessie often gave her.

"It's so cute the way you wear the same thing all the time . . . in three sizes too big. Not like all the other girls in Beverly Hills, who are always worrying about their appearance. You're above that. It's refreshing."

"Thanks, Chessie," Elle said again.

"*Francesca*. And Laurette, people in this town buy so many clothes! Someone has to wear their old castoffs," Chessie said. "You're, like, a living, breathing paragon of recycling."

Laurette looked down at her brightly colored thrift-store dress, which she loved. "Whoever threw this out was crazy."

"I know," Chessie said. "Nineteen seventy-seven was a vintage year for garish polyester. See you in gym." She closed her locker and minced away, taking tiny steps in her miniskirt and high-heeled sandals, her blonde hair gleaming in the fluorescent light.

"It's funny," Elle said. "I want to like her, but for some reason, I don't."

"Maybe because she's a big fake," Laurette pointed out.

"She's never actually done anything mean to me," Elle said.

"She's not nice," Laurette said.

"What did she say that wasn't nice?" Elle said. "She complimented both our outfits—"

"But she didn't mean it," Laurette said.

"How do you know for sure?" Elle said. "Maybe she's just not good at expressing herself. I won't believe she's not nice until she does something mean. Something I can point to and say, 'That was heinous.' Innocent until proven guilty and all that." Elle believed in seeing the best in people wherever possible. Laurette was more cynical.

The bell rang. They headed in to their first class, homeroom, with Ms. Zeller. Elle scouted the room for a good place for her and Laurette to sit, preferably two seats together. Sidney Ugman lurked nearby, waiting for her to sit down before choosing his own seat, which was inevitably as close to Elle as possible.

Elle tried to be nice to Sidney. She tried to like him. But he made it very hard.

She spotted two seats wedged in between Alicia's and David's. She grabbed Laurette by the hand, and they dashed to the seats. Safe! But then Alicia got up and moved, to be closer to Kyra.

Sidney zeroed in. "Hi, Elle," Sidney said. The smell of bologna wafted over her as he sat down. "Guess what I brought for lunch today?"

"Um, I don't know," Elle said. "Bologna?"

Sidney laughed as if this were their intimate running joke. "You guess that every time. No, it's better than that."

"Liverwurst?"

"Wrong again," Sidney said. "Tongue! On rye, with mustard."

Elle's stomach turned. "Yum."

"I'll share it with you if you sit with me at lunch," Sidney said.

"I'm a vegetarian," Elle said, quickly making up an excuse.

Ms. Zeller announced that there would be a pep rally for the boys' varsity basketball team at two o'clock that afternoon. Someone in the back of the room booed and hissed. The basketball team wasn't very popular, probably because the team was terrible.

"All right! No geometry," Laurette whispered.

"This will not be a free period," Ms. Zeller said. "You are all expected to go to the rally. The basketball team needs some support."

"Yeah. Jock support," a boy said from the back of the room. Probably the same boy who had booed. A few people giggled.

Ms. Zeller ignored him. "And if you happen to be in the area this evening, it would be nice if a few Beverly Hills High students dropped by the gym to take in a game for once."

Sidney shook his head. "Nothing more pathetic than a bunch of jocks, am I right?" Chubby Sidney was about as far from athletic as a person could be.

"I feel sorry for them," Elle said.

"So do I," Sidney said sarcastically. "Poor tall, strong, muscular guys. Bunch of freaks."

Elle peered at Sidney through her big glasses.

He grinned at her. "Elle, will you go to the movies with me tonight?" he asked.

"Sorry, I can't," Elle said. He asked her out practically every other day.

"Please? It's my birthday."

"I thought last Friday was your birthday," Elle said.

"I have a lot of birthdays," Sidney replied.

At two o'clock everyone filed into the auditorium. Elle and Laurette found seats together. Before Elle realized what was happening, Sidney was in the seat next to her.

"Give me a *B*!"

Savannah Shaw, the tall, beautiful, blonde head cheerleader, tried to work the crowd into a frenzy of pep. But the pep just wasn't there.

"Give me a *B*!" she called again, louder this time. A few people listlessly repeated, *"B."* Some of the other cheerleaders weren't even paying attention.

Chessie, who was also a cheerleader, jumped up and down and shook her pom-poms. "Woo-hoo! Come on, people! We've got a game to win tonight! Go, Beverly!" Then she accidentally stepped on her own toe and cried, "Ow!"

Two other cheerleaders absently shook their

pom-poms without pausing in the conversation they were having. One girl was talking on her cell phone. Another was filing her nails. The members of the basketball team, in their blue-and-gold uniforms, stood lined up on the stage in the auditorium, waiting for the pep rally to be over.

Savannah dropped her arms. "You people are pathetic. I give up." She sat down on the stage. Chessie, imitating her, sat down, too.

Ms. Mikulski, the principal, took the microphone. "Okay! Let's hear it for the Beverly Hills cheerleaders!" *Clap, clap, clap.* Only one person was clapping, and it was obviously ironic applause.

"Why do they make us come to these things?" Laurette asked. "Why do they bother?"

"It really is sad," Elle said. "Blue and gold look so pretty together, too."

Ms. Mikulski cleared her throat. "Okay. Thank you all for coming today. I know it was required, but . . . Anyway, our Beverly Bluefins have a big game tonight against the Santa Monica Speedsters, and we need all the support we can get. So come on out and cheer for those Bluefins! We've got popcorn, soda, and plenty of hot dogs for your enjoyment! And two kinds of candy."

"You can get better food at the movies," Laurette said.

"And now the captain of the team would like to say a few words," Ms. Mikulski said. "Give it up for the best starting forward Beverly has seen in decades! Hunter Perry!"

There was some genuine applause, and a few girls squealed as a tall boy got to his feet and approached the microphone. The blue-and-gold uniform glinted on his frame like a royal robe. Elle gasped at the sight of him. A light flashed before her eyes. She had a premonition that from that moment on, her life would never be the same.

"Elle? What's the matter?" Laurette asked.

Elle couldn't speak.

Hunter was broad-shouldered, slim-hipped, with thick, glossy, blue-black hair, a high forehead, and long-lashed, dark blue eyes.

"He's beautiful," Elle said. She could see why Hunter was the captain. He was different from the other players. He was taller, stronger, smarter, hand-somer. He was a god. He seemed to glow.

"Look," Hunter said, speaking into the micro-phone. His voice was low and smooth. "I know you don't care about basketball. I know you think we suck."

Ms. Mikulski flashed him a disapproving glare, but he didn't flinch. "But just think about it for a minute. This is your school. We are your team. And you treat us like we're a big joke. Maybe you'd rather play racquetball, or surf, or whatever. I know you'd rather watch pro basketball on TV, or sit courtside with all the celebrities."

The audience began to tune out, except for a few rapt girls and Elle, the raptest of all.

"I understand that. But I play my heart out every game," Hunter said. "I'm trying to win, I really am. I'm doing this for you. For all of us. But I can't do it alone. We need a reason to win. We need people to come and root for us. If we felt like the school was behind us, I swear we could win a few games. We might even have a shot at the championship."

Elle listened to Hunter speak, her heart swelling at every word. Hunter was the best player the school had seen in years—everybody said so. But Beverly Hills High students were rich kids, good at tennis and skiing and horseback-riding. If they wanted to watch basketball, they could get court-side seats for the Lakers. They didn't have to waste their time on a third-rate high-school team. They had better things to do.

Elle thought that that was a shame. She could see the pain on Hunter's face. He was a true athlete, and he wanted to play on a competitive team, where people cared about the sport. He was a senior, and this was his last season. All he was asking for was a little support. But at Beverly Hills, it was every student for himself. Where was the school spirit? Where was the sense of community?

"We can win this year," Hunter said, his voice rising, "if we can just get excited. So let's hear it. Go, Bluefins!"

Savannah and Chessie jumped up and shouted, "Go, Bluefins!"

"Go, Bluefins!" a few female voices cried. But most of the students weren't moved. They just didn't care.

"Hunter Perry." Elle breathed the name. "From this moment on, I live for Hunter Perry. Laurette, I'm in love."

"So is half the school, in case you hadn't noticed," Laurette said. "The female half."

"I don't care," Elle said. "That boy was born to be my Prom date."

"What?"

"You heard me," Elle said. "I am going to the Senior Prom this year. As Hunter's date."

"You're kidding, right?" Laurette said.

Elle pushed her glasses up on her nose. "No. I'm perfectly serious."

"Well, how do you plan to accomplish this miracle?" Laurette asked.

"His speech was a cry for help," Elle said. "It reached me. I must answer."

"*O*-kay." Laurette looked doubtful. "But how? Are you secretly a genius basketball coach?"

"No. I'm going to fill those bleachers with cheering fans. The basketball team will turn its season around when they see that the school cares about them. They're going to win the C-Conference championship. And when Hunter realizes what I've done for him, he'll fall to his knees and beg me to go to the Prom with him."

"Wow," Laurette said. "If all that happens, it *will* be a miracle."

"Is this about the uniform?" Sidney said, suddenly jumping into their conversation. "Because I can get one of those."

"No," Elle said. "It's not about the uniform." It was something bigger. It was True Love.

Chapter 2

WHEN THE pep rally broke up, Elle felt herself drawn by a mysterious force toward the stage, to Hunter.

"What are you going to say to him?" Laurette asked, tagging along behind her.

"I don't know," Elle said. "I'm hoping inspiration will strike me just in time."

Hunter was surrounded by a group of cooing cheerleaders, including Chessie.

"I don't know what everybody's problem is," Chessie said to Hunter. "I'll never miss a game as long as you're playing."

"You *have* to be at every game," Chloe, another cheerleader, said as she elbowed Chessie out of the way. "You're a cheerleader."

"Well, why don't you girls get some of your friends to come to the Friday-night games?" Hunter asked.

"I've tried," Chessie said. "They all say they don't have time."

"Friday night is half off cover charge at Pacifico," Chloe said, naming a club that was hot that month. "Everybody has to be there."

"I know—I go after the game every Friday," Hunter said. "I don't see why your friends can't do that, too. Pacifico doesn't start hopping until after eleven."

"They don't have time," Chloe said. "They have to get dressed to go out. That can take hours."

"And they need to take their disco naps," Rachel pointed out, looking down at her pom-poms.

"They're so vain," Chloe added, admiring the way her new gold bracelet dangled from her bony wrist.

Elle stood off to the side, watching and listening unnoticed. She thought Hunter looked pained, and took the opportunity to move in. She planted herself at his right, opposite Chloe and Chessie. "Hi, Hunter," she said.

He half turned his head, not really looking at her. She grinned a big, metal-mouth smile at him and pushed her glasses up on her nose.

"Hi," he said.

"What if they moved the games to Tuesdays?" Chessie said, drawing Hunter's attention away from Elle. "Hardly anything good happens on Tuesday."

"*The Beach* is on Tuesday nights," Chloe said. "That's why nobody goes out that night."

"Hi," Elle said again, hoping to get Hunter's attention back.

"The rally's over, Elle," Chessie said. "Thank you for coming. We're talking team business now."

"That's what I want to talk about, too," Elle said. Hunter started to turn toward her again, but a girl named Jenna said, "Hunter, your speech was so touching. Really, like, you almost had me in tears."

"He's good at that," Savannah said. "Making girls cry." She was standing a little to the side of Hunter and his cheerleader groupies. She had her own groupies—five basketball players—but she clearly had an ear trained on Hunter's conversation.

"You haven't cried since you were in diapers," Hunter said in a snappy but not mean way. "If then."

"Not over a boy, anyway," Savannah said.

Elle backed away and joined Laurette, who was standing in the wings. Whenever she tried to get Hunter's attention, another girl pulled him away.

And nothing about her seemed to appeal to him strongly enough to overshadow those other girls.

"Were Savannah and Hunter a couple?" Elle asked Laurette.

"School royalty," Laurette said. "For almost two years. They broke up last fall. You never saw them swanning around in his Mercedes convertible?"

Elle vaguely remembered seeing a silver car swish around the school parking lot. "Maybe—"

"It was like they were constantly starring in their own private homecoming parade," Laurette said. "Where were you, on planet Elle? How did you miss it? Sometimes I can't believe how clueless you are about that stuff."

"Not anymore," Elle said. "From now on I'm going to notice everything."

Savannah's voice rang out. "Chessie, gather up the pom-poms," she ordered, and Chessie reluctantly tore herself away from Hunter's side.

"Are we having pregame practice this afternoon, Savannah?" Chessie asked.

"I guess we'd better," Savannah said. "Make sure everybody knows about it."

"I will."

"Look how Chessie sucks up to Savannah," Elle said. "That's not like her. She's usually so—so—"

"Bratty?" Laurette suggested.

"I was going to say sure of herself," Elle said. She watched the group more carefully. Savannah was clearly the boss, the queen bee. And Hunter obviously liked the cheerleaders. Did he like anyone in particular? Elle couldn't tell. None of them really stood out, next to Savannah. They were all slim and athletic and pretty, and mostly blonde. But none of them had Savannah's supernatural magnetism.

"I wonder why they broke up," Elle said.

Laurette shrugged. "Who knows? Savannah Shaw and Hunter Perry don't exactly confide in me. Come on, let's get out of here."

"Wait a minute," Elle said. She looked at Savannah more closely. She might be the key to reaching Hunter, Elle thought. Savannah had to know him well if they'd been together almost two years. And if he had dated her that long, he must have liked that kind of girl, at least a little.

"If I'm going to help the team, I need to get close to them somehow," Elle said, thinking out loud. "I need access. And the girls who have the most access to the boys' basketball team are the cheerleaders."

"So, what, you're going to be a cheerleader now?" Laurette said. "You can't, Elle, not this year.

It's too late. They had tryouts last fall, and the squad is fixed."

"All right, maybe I can't be a cheerleader myself," Elle said. "But I can help them."

"Help them?" Laurette said. "How? And why would they listen to you, anyway? You don't know anything about cheerleading."

"No, but they all listen to Savannah," Elle said. "If I can get her on my side, I'll have the whole team in my hand. And I bet Savannah is a lot like Hunter. She's the head cheerleader, but the squad is lame. Those girls don't really care about cheerleading. They just like to say they're cheerleaders. But I think Savannah would rather be the head of a good squad, one she can be proud of, than a bunch of whiny princesses who can barely be bothered to shake their pom-poms."

"So, you're going to improve the cheerleading squad *and* the basketball team," Laurette said. "Even though you don't know anything about either of them."

"Right," Elle said. She wasn't easily discouraged. "I'll get to Hunter through the cheerleading squad. What do you think?"

"Well, it's crazy," Laurette said. "But as a social experiment, it's irresistible. You, Elle Woods, one of the least cheerleady girls at Beverly Hills, are going to infiltrate them, earn their trust, learn their secrets, and use them to your advantage? This I've got to see."

Elle left the auditorium without saying anything to Savannah. This operation had to be handled delicately. On her way out she spotted Matt Reiss, the student manager of the basketball team. She could tell he was the manager because, even though he wore a uniform, he was short, with pencil-thin arms. Also, on the back of his uniform, it said: MATT REISS, MANAGER.

"Matt? I'm Elle Woods."

Matt stopped and stared at her through glasses even thicker than her own. "Hi?" he said uncertainly.

"Hi. Listen, it's hard being the team manager, isn't it?" Elle said. "I mean, I don't know, but I can imagine it is."

"Well, I'm not wild about laundry duty," Matt said. "And those guys never say thank you."

"They don't? Just as I thought. They don't say thank you. It's the definition of a thankless job! You know what you need? You need an assistant."

"I guess that would be nice, but who would want to be my assistant?"

"I would."

He stared at her again, chewing on some gum. "You would? Why?"

"Because I want to help," Elle said. "I think our team could be really great, and I want to contribute in any way I can."

"You do? Do you know what my job is?"

"Not really," Elle said. "What do you do?"

"I take care of the equipment, I keep score, I clean up the locker room after the team is done trashing it, and I keep track of the schedule."

"Sounds divine," Elle said. "When can I start?"

Matt shrugged. "Whenever you want."

"Great!" She shook Matt's hand. "I'm thrilled to be the new assistant manager."

"You're pretty easily thrilled," Matt said.

Chapter 3

"THE OLD uniforms were so blah." Elle was in the art studio, showing Laurette the new school sports logo she had just designed. They were supposed to be painting watercolors of the saddest moments of their lives—all around them, the deaths of many pets were being faithfully depicted—but Elle didn't have time for that. And anyway, Ms. Rodman, the art teacher, wasn't very strict.

"Right now it's a gold *B* over a picture of a bluefin tuna," Elle said. "I mean, I don't know, a fish? Somehow that doesn't say 'winner' to me. It's not exactly glamorous."

"I totally agree," Laurette said.

"So what do you think of this?" Elle unveiled her

design. It showed the Beverly *B* in gold sequins with a crown on top, surrounded by fuzzy golden bumblebees. "Do you love it?"

"It's adorable," Laurette said. "But isn't the *B* supposed to stand for 'Bluefins'?"

"I think we should change our team name," Elle said. "Bluefins? What is that? A kind of sushi. What message are we sending the other teams when we come out and say we're sushi? That they're going to eat us raw."

"I never thought of that," Laurette said. "But you're right. The bluefin is not a very threatening mascot."

"That's why I think we should change our name to the Killer Bees," Elle said. "Bees sting. Killer bees cause major damage. It's so much tougher than 'Bluefin.' But at the same time, bumblebees are pretty and golden. So we get the best of both worlds. Plus, you know, *B*, for Beverly Hills . . . *B* for bee. They're the same. Get it?"

"Duh, no, I don't get it." Laurette gave Elle a smug look.

"Quit kidding around. Do you think Savannah will like it?"

"*I* like it," Laurette said. "If Savannah has any

brains behind her perfectly plucked eyebrows, she'll like it, too. But I don't know for sure that she does have brains."

"She must," Elle said. "Hunter would never fall for a girl who wasn't smart."

"How do you know? You just met the guy for the first time an hour ago. And he didn't even say hi to you."

"He would have, but he was distracted," Elle said. "Anyway, I just know. A girl knows these things when she's in love."

"All of a sudden you're an expert," Laurette said.

"I told you, that rally changed my life forever," Elle said.

"Elle and Laurette?" Ms. Rodman came to their table to see what they were up to. "How are your watercolors coming?"

Elle hadn't worked on anything but the logo, and Laurette had drawn a picture of a TV screen with the words DAWSON'S CREEK IS CANCELED scrawled across it. Ms. Rodman frowned.

"Elle, can you explain your sad moment to me?"

"Sure," Elle said. "I can understand why you wouldn't get it right away, because it's symbolic. The *B* stands for 'blue,' as in sad. And the bees represent my tears—tears that sting."

"But what was the moment that made you sad?" Ms. Rodman asked.

"It hasn't happened yet," Elle said. She imagined the saddest moment she could think of, so sad that tears sprang to her eyes. She was thinking of a Senior Prom where Hunter was another girl's date. "And I hope it never will."

"Hmmm," Ms. Rodman said. "It's not quite what I assigned. Keep working."

"Beverly rules! All the schools! Taber's just a bunch of tools! Go, Bluefins!"

"You guys forgot the clapping thing at the end," Savannah said. "Come on, can't you get even this cheer right? It's totally simple."

Elle hovered in the doorway of the gym watching the cheerleaders practice, clutching her logo design in her hand. One girl's cell phone rang in the middle of a cheer. She stopped to answer it.

"This is lame," Jenna said. "Can't we do a more interesting cheer? Something that really says who we are. Like, *Beverly Hills, the place to be. No one else has more mon-ey! You're just losers, you're just slobs. Go ahead and call us snobs. Yay, us!*"

Savannah shook her head. "Jenna, this is about sports. We're supposed to get people excited about the game! That's our job!"

"Well, if we make the other team feel insecure, maybe they'll blow it," Jenna said.

"Good strategy," Savannah said sarcastically.

"Yeah, good strategy, Jenna," Chessie said.

"Does anyone else have any brilliant ideas?" Savannah said. "We've got a game tonight, you know."

"I do, Savannah," Chessie said. "The team is called the Bluefins, right? So why don't we do a fish formation? Like, wiggle our tails and spray water on the other team? We could even wear fins on our heads. Or flippers."

Savannah crossed her arms and stared at Chessie. "That would make us look totally ridiculous."

Chessie's face fell.

"But at least you're thinking," Savannah added. "Come on, girls. I don't want to wish I were cheering with a paper bag on my head. Let's not embarrass ourselves like last week."

"It's not really that embarrassing," Chloe said. "Hardly anybody comes to see us."

Savannah sighed. "Just show up by seven." The rehearsal broke up, and the cheerleaders scattered.

"I'll pick up the pom-poms," Chessie volunteered, heading for the pile on the floor.

Savannah sat down on a bleacher and stared at a cheer sheet. This was Elle's chance.

"Savannah," Elle said.

"What?" Savannah snapped.

Uh-oh. Foul mood.

"I have something to show you," Elle said, waving the sketch like a white flag. "It's just an idea, but—"

Savannah snatched the sketch and glared at it. Slowly her expression softened. "It's pretty," she said. "What is it?"

"A new logo for your uniforms," Elle said. "It's just an idea, but I thought a new logo might perk everybody up."

"Let me see." Chessie ran over and peered over Savannah's shoulder. "It's cute, Elle. Reminds me of a cartoon. For kids. But that's really popular, you know, in some places. Like kindergarten. Too bad we can't use it."

"I like it," Savannah said. "But why did you draw all these bees? We're the Bluefins."

"Yeah, it's really not right for us," Chessie said.

"Bees are prettier," Elle said.

"I can't argue with that," Savannah said.

"They *are* sweet," Chessie said.

"But they also sting," Elle said. "And bluefin—it's tuna. It gets eaten. I think that sends the wrong message. Like, just chop us into bite-size pieces with a little wasabi on the side."

"Oh, Elle," Chessie said. "This isn't about food. It's about basketball. *Basketball.*"

"Elle's right," Savannah said. "I never thought about it that way. How did we ever get named the Bluefins, anyway? Didn't we used to be the Bulls?"

"I think it was a few years ago, when sushi became so popular," Chessie said. "Somebody must have thought it was chic."

"Chessie, could you leave us alone for a minute?" Elle said, getting a sudden burst of bravery. "I need to talk to Savannah."

"I'm the junior head cheerleader," Chessie said. "Whatever you have to say, I should hear it."

"Chessie, go put the pom-poms away," Savannah said.

Chessie skulked away slowly.

"I'm glad you like the sketch," Elle said. "I can make new logos over the weekend and sew them onto everyone's uniform by next Friday."

"Excellent," Savannah said. "Why are you doing this?"

"Because I care," Elle said. "And I can tell that you care, too. This squad needs help, Savannah. It's a shame. So much talent, going to waste."

"What can I do about it?" Savannah said. "No one comes to see us, so the girls don't care what we do."

"But if the cheerleaders were great, people would come," Elle said. "And that would help the basketball team, too. I know this squad can be better. It can be more. And I can turn it around."

Chessie returned from the equipment closet and hovered nearby, listening.

"How can you do that?" Savannah asked. "You don't look like a cheerleader."

"I'm not," Elle said. "But I can spot a squad in trouble when I see it."

"Elle, you're sweet to want to help," Chessie said. "But you don't know squat about cheerleading. Or much of anything. No offense."

"What's your plan, exactly?" Savannah asked.

Inside, Elle was squirming. She didn't have a plan. She had no ideas. Nothing. But that wouldn't stop her. She'd just get some. They were out there somewhere. All she had to do was find them.

"It's too complicated to go into now," Elle said. "I'll come watch you at the game tonight, so I know exactly what the problems are. Then let's have lunch on Monday and I'll explain all my ideas."

"Elle, come on," Chessie said. "Look at you. Your glasses, your braces, your mousy hair . . . There's not a cheerleading bone in your body. What could you show us that we don't already know?"

Savannah stared at her skeptically. "Yes, what?"

"You'll just have to trust me," Elle said. "Look at it this way: you can meet me for lunch and listen to my plan, or you can keep doing the same lame routines until you graduate, having wasted your precious high-school years. What will it be?"

"Elle," Chessie said. "I know you mean well, but Savannah doesn't have time to—"

"Quiet, Chessie," Savannah said. "She's got guts. All right—what was your name again?"

"Elle."

"I'll meet you for lunch on Monday. But you had better have some good ideas." She sounded stern, but she smiled at Elle.

"Yeah, they'd better be good," Chessie echoed.

"They will be," Elle promised.

"Muffins for my little Ellie." Zosia Wytzowski, the Woodses' maid, wiggled onto the back terrace with a plate of muffins and a pitcher of milk. She was in her late twenties, petite and curvy, with curly brown hair and big blue eyes that always looked surprised—but not *that* surprised. She wore a short, pale blue uniform with a frilly white apron that nipped in at the waist. "I made them with oatmeal, bran, and special oils to give your skin an extra-shiny glow."

"Thanks, Zosia."

"And don't forget the milk," Zosia said. "The special oils combine with milk to make your hair glossy." Zosia liked to make her own homemade cosmetics and had a vast knowledge of natural beauty secrets. It was the main reason Elle's mother had hired her.

Zosia picked up a limp hank of Elle's hair and frowned. "I suppose glossy and mousy is better than just plain mousy."

Elle pushed her glasses up on her nose. "I bet after I eat this muffin, my hair will shine like a new penny."

"Hmmm . . ." Zosia said doubtfully. "Your glasses are too big for you. You're always sliding them up your nose. It's not ladylike."

"Not much I can do about that," Elle said. "I can't see without them."

"What about contact lenses?" Zosia said. She was

32

always pushing the idea of contacts for Elle. "Your eyes are so beautiful. The world should see them!"

"We tried that, remember?" Elle said. Elle's mother had bought her a pair of contacts, and Elle had tried to put them in, but they'd stung her eyes and made them water. "I could hardly see! And I looked like I was crying all the time."

"But that was ages ago," Zosia said. "They have new ones now. Better ones. I'll help you. I know a few tricks to keep them comfortable. Look!" She batted her long eyelashes to show off her bright, pool–blue contact lenses.

"Someday soon," Elle said. "Right now I'm too busy."

"You always say you're too busy," Zosia said. "What are you up to now?"

"I've got to go to a basketball game tonight. And then I'm going to spend the weekend learning everything I can about cheerleading."

"You? At a basketball game?" Zosia said.

"Yes, and it starts at seven, so I have to eat dinner early," Elle said. "What are we having tonight?"

"I don't know," Zosia said. "Ask Lurch over there." She nodded at Bernard, the butler, who was walking back from the garden with a basket full of peonies. He was extremely tall—six foot seven—with gray-black hair, bushy black eyebrows, and a lantern jaw. He smiled at Elle and stuck a pink flower in her hair.

"Thank you, Bernard," Elle said. "I have to eat at six tonight. Can we have eggplant Parmesan again?"

"Whatever makes you happy, miss," Bernard said. "I'll tell madam you won't be dining with her tonight."

"Unless she feels like eating early," Elle said.

"Unlikely, miss," Bernard said. Elle's parents never ate dinner before eight P.M. "But perhaps she'll sit with you and fuss over you while you eat."

"Yes, perhaps she will," Elle said.

"For sure she will," Zosia said.

"Jump ball! Jump ball! Get it! Get it!"

The cheerleaders shouted as Hunter faced off against the Santa Monica forward. He jumped for the ball and slapped it to John Fourier, a Beverly Hills teammate. The ball slipped out of John's hands as if it were greased with butter and bounced on the floor. A Santa Monica Speedster swiped it and dribbled it down the court for a basket.

"Hunter might as well be out there alone for all the help he's getting from the rest of the team," Elle said to Laurette.

The score at the end of the first half was 19–2. A cheer went up in the visitors' bleachers.

"They've got more spectators than we have," Laurette said. "And this is a home game for us."

Elle glanced around at the empty stands. The visitors had brought maybe thirty fans. The home team had a few devoted parents in the front row, and about five girls sprinkled throughout the rest of the bleachers, including Elle and Laurette.

"This is even sadder than I expected," Elle said.

Halftime. The Speedsters' cheerleaders ran onto the court in their shiny red-and-white vinyl uniforms with racing-car logos on them.

"Those are hot," Laurette said.

"We're mighty, we're crazy, we're never, ever lazy," the Speedster girls chanted while bouncing and doing backflips all over the place. *"We'll beat you, defeat you, we'll even try to eat you! Yum, yum, we love Bluefin! Go, Speedsters! Yay!"*

"Even *they're* on to the sushi thing," Elle said. "We've got to change our mascot—that's the first thing." She underlined it in her notebook.

"Uh-oh, here come the sneer-leaders," Laurette said.

Savannah trotted onto center court, followed by Chessie. The other girls still sat on their bench, preening and checking their hair. They hadn't even noticed it was halftime.

"Stand up!" Savannah stamped her foot and shouted, not to the crowd but to her own cheerleaders. "Stand *up!*" She and Chessie started cheering while the other girls shambled onto the court. *"We're number one! Under the sun! As for you— you're number two! Ick! P-U! You stink! Yay!"*

Need new cheers, Elle wrote in her notebook.

They did a simple step-clap routine, no fancy flips or jumps, just a final basket toss at the end. Chessie and Savannah threw Chloe high into the air. Chessie nearly let her fall on her way down. Then they all jumped up and down, and Rachel's hair ribbon got caught on Chessie's bracelet.

"Ow! Chessie!" Rachel grabbed her ponytail to keep Chessie from yanking on it. Savannah intervened, pulling Chessie's bracelet off and untangling it from Rachel's hair.

People in the stands shouted, "Boo!" and "You suck!"

"It's really sad when your own fans boo you," Laurette said.

The final score was 56–18. Hunter scored every one of the Beverly points, mostly off foul shots. The Speedsters left in triumph. The few Beverly

Hills spectators filed out of the gym, dispirited. Elle watched Hunter as he stood on the court alone, dribbling the ball and practicing free throws. Every single one swished in. But he didn't look happy.

"Come on, Elle," Matt Reiss called. "We've got work to do."

"Time to start my new assistant-manager duties," Elle said to Laurette. "I'll call you later."

She passed Hunter on the court. "Good game," she said. It hadn't been a good game, but what else could she say?

He didn't even look at her but just grimly threw the ball again. *Swish.*

"You're a star among tunas," Elle said.

Chapter 4

"HONEY, WHAT are you doing in there?" Elle's mother knocked on the door, then opened it without waiting for permission. Elle was used to that. She was sitting on her bed watching *Bring It On* for the third time in a row. Those movie cheerleaders had some moves, she thought. Even their lamest routines looked pretty good to her.

"It's Saturday afternoon, the sun is shining on southern California in all its glory!" Eva said. "Come on out by the pool for a while and get some sun." She took Elle's chin in her palm and studied her face. "You must be the palest girl in L.A. Honey, I'm telling you, it's strange to see a girl look so sallow in this climate. Creepy. You are beginning to look a lot like Wednesday Addams."

"I've got too much to do," Elle said. "Go away." She propped her elbow on a tall stack of cheerleading magazines and books.

"It's not like you to watch so much TV," Eva said.

"I'm not watching TV. I'm studying," Elle said.

"At least get dressed! You're still in your pj's!"

Wyatt popped in, dressed in spiffy tennis whites, twirling a racket. "Up for a game, pussycat? I learned a new service technique at the club this morning. I'll blow aces past you so fast they'll singe your eyebrows."

"Leave her eyebrows alone," Eva said. "They're a mess as it is."

Elle was busy jotting down cheerleading terminology. "Sorry, Dad, no time for tennis," she said. "Can everyone please get out of my room now? I'm trying to concentrate."

"She won't come out," Eva said. "She's glued to the TV for some reason."

"It's important," Elle said. "I only have—" She glanced at the alarm clock on her night table. "—Forty-four more hours to learn everything there is to know about cheerleading."

"But who will I play tennis with?" Wyatt asked. "I hate hitting the ball against the wall all by myself."

"I'll play a set with you, darling," Eva said.

"But you're terrible," Wyatt said. "You're so afraid you'll break a nail you never give the ball a good whack. That's why I love to play with Elle—she's a great whacker."

"Another time, Dad," Elle said.

"I'm afraid it's me or the wall, Wyatt," Eva said. "Honestly, our daughter is getting weirder by the day."

Finally, they left her in peace. A few minutes later, Bernard appeared with a tray. "I've brought you your lunch, miss," he said. "And your friend."

Laurette clapped her hands in the doorway. "*L-A-U-R-E-T-T*. At the end you have an *E*. It's me! Laurette! Yay!"

Bernard set Elle's lunch tray on a table. "Would you like some lunch?" he asked Laurette.

"Sure," Laurette said. She peeked at the grilled-cheese sandwich on Elle's tray. "I'll have what she's having."

"Fine." He left for the kitchen, taking Elle's empty breakfast tray with him. Laurette bounced onto the bed next to Elle, who had finished with *Bring It On* and was now watching an instructional cheerleading video.

A small squad of college girls demonstrated different stunts. "Herkie to a pike, then round-off back tuck," the coach instructed as the girls did impossible-looking tricks. Elle stared at the screen, trying to take in all the unfamiliar information. "Torches go into a Liberty as the flier goes into an x-out basket toss."

"You know what the difference between these girls and the Beverly Hills squad is?" Laurette asked.

"What?"

"These girls don't suck."

"Laurette! I'm trying to stay positive."

"I just don't see Chessie flying into the air and somersaulting like that. Someone could get killed. I mean, someone besides Chessie."

"That's okay," Elle said. "Because everyone has different positions, and some girls never leave the ground. They're called bases. Chessie will be a base. Our team isn't organized well enough. That's point number one." She showed Laurette her notebook, where her plan was beginning to take shape.

Bernard reappeared and quietly set down the second grilled-cheese sandwich. He stood watching the video for a few seconds. "I've seen better," he said. "When you're ready for smoothies, just give me a *B*."

"Thanks, Bernard."

"So you're holing up in here for the whole weekend, until cheer leaks out of your brain?" Laurette asked.

"Yep."

"Not even a movie break tonight with your old pal L?"

"Not unless you want to watch a cheerleading movie," Elle said.

"I admire your stamina," Laurette said. "I'd have lost it already. How can you stand all this pep?"

"Luckily, I have Bernard to keep me supplied with meals, snacks, and moral support," Elle said. "And Zosia comes in and gives me a quick shoulder rub every few hours."

"You *are* lucky," Laurette said. She tasted her sandwich and added, "Plus, Bernard makes the best grilled cheese in town."

By Monday morning, Elle felt dazed but ready for her lunch with Savannah. Maybe she couldn't actually do any stunts herself, but she knew enough cheerleading terminology to talk about it, at least.

"Are you all right?" Sidney asked her in the hallway on the way to lunch. The bologna smell had preceded him. "Your eyes are all red."

"I'm okay," Elle said. "I just spent too many hours staring at the TV screen."

"I get that when I play Deathmonger for too long," Sidney said. "Want to borrow my eyedrops?"

"That's okay."

"So . . . I see we're both walking in the direction of the cafeteria," Sidney said.

"Looks that way."

"I happen to be free for lunch today."

"Sorry, Sidney, but I have to talk to someone."

"Actually, so do I," Sidney said. He turned toward a table full of band geeks. "Top secret band business."

"Have fun." Elle spotted Savannah alone at the "cool" table and went over to her.

"Make it quick, Elle," Savannah said. "I've got a date with destiny outside." She looked out the window at a very hot guy twirling a lacrosse stick. "When Hurricane Savannah comes ashore, he won't know what hit him. Expect major damage. By the time I'm done with him, he'll be calling for the National Guard."

Elle didn't know what to say. She had never known anyone who talked that way about herself before. But Savannah seemed to expect some kind of response.

"You sure are sure of yourself," Elle said. As soon as the words tripped out of her mouth she wanted to swallow them back. She could have kicked herself for sounding so stupid. Why did she have to be so blunt?

Savannah smiled. "You're right. I am. So, what's the big plan?"

"Okay. We've got a long way to go, but we've got to start somewhere, right?" Elle said. "So, first—organize. Assign each girl a position. Bigger girls are bases, smaller girls are fliers. The strongest girls are spotters. That way each girl only has to learn the skills that go with her position."

"Yeah. And—?"

"The stunts have to be more spectacular. They have to make people say, 'Ooh!' More tosses, more jumps, more flips. Right now you're just doing a lot of stamping and clapping."

"That's going to take some practice."

"You guys can do it! I know you can."

"Anything else?" Savannah asked.

"Yes. The cheers themselves. They need to be cleverer, and more connected to the game and what's happening on the court. I've written a few new ones you could try—"

"Is this seat taken?" Chessie sat down with her tray. She was wearing a robin's-egg-blue tank top just like one that Savannah had worn the week before. Elle had noticed it because it was such a pretty color.

"Elle, what's the matter? You look terrible! You poor thing, you'd better go to the nurse right away."

"I'm just a little bleary," Elle said. "I'll be all right."

"A little bleary?" Chessie said. "Savannah, don't you think she looks positively wretched?"

"Quiet, Chessie, we're in the middle of something." Savannah skimmed Elle's sample cheers. Chessie leaned over to sneak a peek.

"These are so funny, Elle," Chessie said. "Really, you should write, like, a cheerleading parody. You know, where everyone thinks the cheers they're yelling are good, but they actually stink? It would be a riot."

"They're not bad," Savannah said, giving Chessie a stern look. "Better than *'You're number two, P-U.'*"

"Well, that is a weak one," Chessie said. "But some of our other cheers are good. What about: *'Caution! Hotcakes coming through!'*?"

"I'm sick of that one," Savannah said.

"Too many of your cheers are about how hot

you are," Elle said.

"Come to practice this afternoon, and see what the other girls think," Savannah said to Elle. "Maybe we can try some of your stunts."

"We don't want to waste Elle's time," Chessie said. "I mean, all this seems silly to me. I'm sure the other girls will agree. And Elle probably has better things to do after school—like chew her nails a little shorter." She flashed Elle a disarmingly sweet smile.

Elle looked at her fingernails. They were ragged and unpolished. She'd never thought about that before.

"No, really, I have time," Elle said. "I want to come."

Chessie opened her mouth to protest, but Savannah said, "Shut up, Chessie. She's coming. See you at three-fifteen, Elle." She got up and went outside to the cute lacrosse player, leaving her tray to be bused by someone— anyone—else.

"I wouldn't bother showing up, Elle, really," Chessie said. "I mean, the season's almost half over. What good can you do now? And next year I'll be head cheerleader, and Hunter will be in college, and I'll go visit him wherever he is and get advice from the cheerleaders there—real ones, who know what they're talking about."

"What do you mean, you'll visit Hunter in college?" Elle asked.

"Well, I'm just assuming we'll be a couple by then," Chessie said. "After I cheer him on all season. Then the Prom . . . You get the picture."

Steam practically came out of Elle's ears. Chessie wanted Hunter, too? Of course—what girl wouldn't? But Elle had never thought of Chessie as direct competition before. And Chessie seemed so sure of everything—as if she knew dating Hunter were really going to happen. Was Savannah helping her somehow? After all, Savannah knew Hunter better than any other girl in school.

All the more reason to stay close to her, Elle thought. And to Hunter, to learn whatever she could. After all, Chessie had said, "*After* he asks me to the Prom." He hadn't asked her yet.

"I think I'll show up anyway," Elle said, keeping her cool. "Just in case."

"Mom? What are you doing here?"

Elle was on her way to the gym when she spotted her mother's Mercedes in the school parking lot.

"You have an appointment at the orthodontist's,

remember?" Eva said. "Come on, we'll be late."

"I can't go," Elle said. "I've got cheerleading practice."

"You're not a cheerleader."

"I know. But I still have to go to practice."

"You can go tomorrow. Get in the car. You're finally getting your braces off! I would think you'd be excited."

Elle stared longingly toward the gym. She was so ready to show those girls what she knew. But then she said, "You're right, Mom. I am excited." She got into the car.

None of those cheerleaders wears braces, Elle thought as the car sped toward the orthodontist's office. And from now on, neither will I. This will bring me one step closer to being like them. Like Savannah. The kind of girl Hunter likes.

She'd rock those cheerleaders' world. But they'd have to wait until tomorrow.

Chapter 5

"YOU GOT your braces off!" Laurette exclaimed the next morning. She leaned close, to get a good look at Elle's teeth. Elle obligingly opened wide. "So white and straight! They look beautiful!"

"Thanks." Elle was glad she'd done it. No more rubber bands. No more food stuck in the tracks. No more icky metal mouth.

"Wow, Elle, you're more stunning than ever," Sidney said. "You look like a supermodel."

Elle adjusted her glasses and tugged on her baggy T-shirt. Her mousy hair was pulled back in a messy ponytail. "Thanks, Sidney."

Hunter and some of his friends rolled by, doing their rule-the-school strut. Elle flashed her newly liberated teeth at him. He smiled back! But he didn't quite catch her eye. Elle followed his gaze and realized he was smiling at Chessie.

"See you at practice this afternoon, Hunter?" Chessie said.

"You know it," Hunter said. "I like to check in on you girls just to bug Savannah."

Chessie giggled.

Elle piped up and said, "I'll be there today, too."

"Elle's kind of like our mascot," Chessie said. "You know how some teams have dogs, or pigs? We have Elle. She's like our team mouse."

Hunter looked confused. "But we're the Bluefins."

"We're going to be the Killer Bees soon," Elle explained. "Only nobody knows it yet."

"Hey, Perry, let's move," one of Hunter's friends called.

"Whatev'," Hunter said, glancing in Elle's direction. "See you."

"Bye, Hunter!" Chessie called.

"Double bye!" Elle shouted.

"You shouldn't be so forward. Boys don't like that." Then Chessie stared at Elle more closely. "There's something different about you."

"I got my braces off."

"Finally. Wow, took you long enough. Most people get theirs off by the end of junior high. I didn't want to tell you before, but they made you look geeky. I'd never say something like that to somebody's face."

"But now I don't look geeky?" Elle asked.

"I didn't say that."

"And this is the new logo I designed." Elle said later that afternoon as she showed Chessie and the other cheerleaders the prototype Killer Bees logo she'd whipped up over the weekend. "I'll have to convince the basketball team to change their logo, too, to match."

"It looks pretty," Chloe said. "But we're the Bluefins."

"I know," Elle said. "But do we have to be? I don't see why we can't be whatever we want."

"So, you're saying you want to change our team name, our logo, and our cheers?" Jenna said. "Isn't this all kind of drastic? And you're not even a cheerleader."

"Yeah, look at her," Rachel said. "Does she even know the first thing about cheering? You can tell by looking at her she's never been one."

"I say we give her ideas a try," Savannah said.

"What have we got to lose?"

"We could look like idiots," Jenna said. "Why should we listen to her? She'd never make it past the first round of a cheerleading tryout. She's just not . . . she's so totally not, you know, a cheerleader."

"That's not true, Jenna," Chessie said. "Anyone can be a cheerleader *inside*. Even if they are totally mousy on the outside."

"I agree with Jenna," Chloe said. "It's not like she's some kind of expert. Why should we listen to her?"

"Because you're stuck in a rut," Elle said, jumping into the conversation. "It's nothing to be ashamed of. It happens to everyone. Sometimes it takes an outsider to come in and see how things can improve."

"Elle's thinking *creatively*," Chessie said. "She's thinking outside the box. Way outside."

The girls laughed. Elle pulled a lock of hair over her face to hide her disappointment. Even with Savannah's support, she was having trouble winning them over. They were so sure of themselves, so sure they knew everything. . . . That was their trouble.

"Look, can we get back to practicing now?"

Rachel said. "This is a waste of time."

"I've never heard you say you wanted to practice before, Rachel," Savannah said. "All right. We'll talk about this, Elle, and take a vote. I'll let you know what we decide. Thanks for trying to help."

Chessie led Elle to the door of the gym. "Yes, thanks, Elle. You're so sweet to try to help us! I know you'd love to be part of the squad, but not many girls have what it takes. Remember—when you come to the games and root for the team, that's cheering! That's doing your part. 'Kay?"

Elle stepped out, and Chessie slammed the gym door shut.

"How can you stand it?" Eva asked. "Aren't you hot, lounging out here in those baggy sweats?"

Elle was sitting by the pool, sketching in her notebook. Zosia had banished her from the kitchen for moping. Elle had filled page after page with sad puppies, sad kittens, and sad clowns.

Her mother took one look at some of the pictures and said, "Did you have a bad day at school?"

"Kind of," Elle said.

"Want to talk about it?"

"Not really."

"Are you wearing sunscreen? You need some

color, but I don't want you to turn into Lobster Girl."

"Being Lobster Girl would be better than being me," Elle said.

"That doesn't sound like my Elle," Eva said. "Something serious must be wrong. You need cheering up. And I know exactly what to do." She took the notebook from Elle's hand and dragged her to her feet. "You're coming with me."

"Where are you taking me?" Elle asked.

"To therapy," Eva said.

"Mom, it isn't that bad."

"Not psychotherapy," Eva said. "My kind of therapy. The kind that actually works. You're getting your first mani-pedi."

Chapter 6

"MOM, THE last thing I want to do is sit around a salon for two hours," Elle said. "I've got so many other things to do."

Eva dragged Elle through a shiny glass door into the Pamperella Salon. Inside, it was cool but happily bustling. A pink-suited receptionist greeted them. Manicurists in pale pink dresses sat in a long row at their tables, talking to clients while they soaked and rubbed and polished their hands. Mysterious doors opened and closed, and women in robes and shower caps came out glowing.

"Trust me, honey. You don't listen to me very often," Eva said. "But if there's one thing I know, it's this: there's nothing a good mani-pedi can't fix. I don't care how busy you are; this is important."

She presented Elle to the receptionist. "Kylie, this is my daughter, Elle. She has virgin nails."

"What? How old is she?" Kylie took Elle's hand and studied it.

"Believe it or not, she's sixteen years old."

"Oh, my. And it's your first time, sweetheart?" Kylie asked Elle. "For real? Or maybe you had a secret manicure you never told Mommy about?"

"Never," Elle said. "I swear."

"You can tell she hasn't," Eva said. "Look at those cuticles."

"Bitten to the quick," Kylie clucked. "For her first time she needs a real pro. Someone gentle. Bibi!" she called to a young woman walking by. "Someone to see you. This is Elle. Virgin nails."

Bibi stopped and took both of Elle's hands in hers. "Welcome, Elle." She had a twang in her voice. "Don't worry, sugar, we'll have a fine time. Come with me."

Eva kissed Elle. "You'll love it! You'll see."

Elle followed Bibi to a table and sat down. Bibi's long, straight, brown hair spilled out from under a baby-blue cowboy hat. A tiny Chihuahua with a bulging stomach waddled up to her and curled around her feet.

"Hey, there, Kitty," Bibi said. "I named her Kitty after Kitty Wells, an old country singer I like. It never even crossed my mind that it might not be a good name for a dog until my boyfriend pointed it out. Calling a dog Kitty! I swear! Sometimes I'm so dumb I make myself dizzy."

Elle laughed and reached down to pet Kitty. "Is she going to have puppies?"

"Real soon," Bibi said. "Won't they be cute? Now give me your hands, let me loosen them up for you."

Elle relaxed as Bibi massaged her fingers. "I can't believe you've never had a manicure before, at your age! I had my first when I was eight! But that's Texas for you. We do everything early down there, when we don't do it late."

"You're from Texas?" Elle asked. "Why did you move here?"

"I wanted to see the world, pick up a little sophistication," Bibi said. "I love it here. Some of my clients are movie stars! They're more fun to talk to than Dallas socialites."

Elle didn't say anything. The hand massage was melting her brain.

"Do you know what color polish you want?"

Bibi asked. "You can pick out anything you like from that display by the window."

"You pick out something," Elle said. "A pretty shade of pink."

"I know the perfect one," Bibi said. "Soak your fingers in this lotion, and I'll be right back."

Bibi picked up Kitty and set her on Elle's lap. "You won't be able to pet her much because your hands will be occupied, but I find it's nice just to have her on my lap, all warm and cozy."

Elle petted Kitty before dipping her fingers in the lotion. Bibi returned with a bottle of pearly pink polish.

"You look like a girl with something on her mind," Bibi said. "Something bothering you? There must be some reason why your mother brought you in here today."

"Actually, there is," Elle said. "But it's a long story."

"Lay it on me, sugar," Bibi said. "We've got nothing but time."

Elle wasn't sure where to start. "My school's cheerleading squad is no good. I spent all weekend coming up with ideas to help them get better, but they won't listen to me."

"Hmmm," Bibi said. "That's a strange problem.

Why do you care that they're bad? One glance at your calf muscles tells me you're not a pepster yourself."

Elle looked down at the scrawny calves poking out of her oversized shorts. "You can tell that just from looking at my legs?"

"Well, that and the glasses. You couldn't get through a decent routine with those things on. They'd go flying into the stands."

Elle was impressed. No matter what Bibi might have said about herself, she was smart. She knew people. She was Elle's kind of woman.

"The reason I care is because I want the basketball team to get better," Elle said. "And they won't get better unless they have more fans. A good cheer squad could bring up attendance."

"Maybe," Bibi said. "But I still don't believe this is the whole story. If this doesn't have something to do with a boy, I'll eat my emery board."

"His name is Hunter," Elle said, "and he's the most incredible guy who ever cruised the streets of Beverly Hills."

"I thought so. This Hunter is a basketball player and you're trying to get his attention?"

Elle nodded. "Are you sure you want to hear this? I never get to talk about him. My best friend,

Laurette, is sick of hearing about him, and I don't have anyone else to confide in."

"Sure, sweetie, I'd like to hear all about him. What's he look like?"

Elle began to rhapsodize over Hunter's hair, his eyes, his shoulders, his smile. The way his hands held the basketball. His finesse every time the ball swished through the net. How perfect he would look taking her to Prom.

"You've got it bad, haven't you, honey?" Bibi said, buffing Elle's nails. "That's okay. There's only one way to fall in love, and that's full throttle."

"Are you in love?" Elle asked.

"Not at the moment," Bibi said, "unless you count Kitty—I'm crazy about her. But I've been there. Trust me, I've been there."

"I have a long way to go," Elle said. "I can't even get Hunter to say hi to me."

Bibi trimmed Elle's chewed-up cuticles. Elle was so engrossed in the conversation she hardly noticed anything was happening to her hands at all.

"That doesn't matter," Bibi said. "We'll start at the beginning. You've got a plan to help those cheerleaders. But they won't listen to you. I can help."

"You can? How?"

"Honey, today is your lucky day," Bibi said.

"Don't you remember I told you I was from Texas? Texas is the cheerleading capital of the galaxy. And you're talking to the former head cheerleader of the Armadillo High Dillies. Just watch this!"

Bibi sprang to her feet and got into position. "Kylie!" she called to the receptionist. "My music, please! Hit it!"

A groovy funk song started thumping through the salon. Everyone looked up at Bibi, who seemed to be holding imaginary pom-poms at her hips.

Ready? Let's go! All you Armadillo fans, let me see you clap your hands! Now that you all got the beat, let me see you stomp your feet! Now that you all got the groove, let me see your body move! Ahuga! Ah! Ah! Ahuga! D-I-L-L-Y! We're the team that makes you cry! Go home, babies, go home now! Here's a kick to show you how!

Bibi did a funky dance routine, ending with a flying kung fu kick right out of a martial-arts film. Activity in the salon stopped in its tracks to watch her. She jumped so high in the air Elle couldn't believe she didn't have springs in her shoes. She did some gymnastics moves Elle didn't even know the name of, then grabbed Elle and tossed her into the air. Elle landed neatly on her shoulders while Bibi slid into a split.

The salon erupted in cheers.

"That was amazing!" Elle said. "You must have been the best cheerleader in Texas."

"Nah, just average," Bibi said. "But I've got plenty more moves I bet those Beverly Hills girls never even dreamed of."

She sat down again. Elle took her place across the table from her. Bibi coolly began to paint the pearly polish on Elle's nails. She wasn't even out of breath.

"I'll teach you that routine," Bibi said. "You show it to those girls and they'll listen to you, I bet."

Elle knew they would. "Thanks, Bibi."

"But there's a lot more to cheering than the moves," Bibi said. "Little things count, too. Hair, uniforms, socks, makeup—everything. The girls have to look alike as much as possible, and perfectly neat. One secret—hair spray, hair spray, hair spray. I know a brand that cements your hair in place. It keeps you neat no matter how crazy your tumbling is."

"Tumbling," Elle said. "These girls don't do any tumbling."

"They'll have to learn," Bibi said. "Don't worry—I'll tell you everything I know."

Elle felt as if she were floating as she left the salon. "You liked it, didn't you?" Eva said as she led her daughter to the car. "I can see it on your face."

Elle admired her beautiful, pearly pink nails. Unburdening herself to Bibi had relaxed her and given her confidence. She felt like a new girl. And she couldn't wait to come back.

"You were right, Mom. I feel great! Why didn't I ever do this before? I think I'll have a manicure every week."

Eva smiled. "So you *are* my daughter, after all."

Chapter 7

"ELLE, YOU guys look so cute in your little kinder-garten outfits," Chessie said. "Was there some kind of theme day or something I didn't know about?"

"These are our cheerleading costumes," Elle said. "Just for today. We didn't have time to find real ones."

"That's good," Chessie said. "Because I've already been Tinker Bell—for Halloween, when I was six. Look, you sewed those cute little bumble-bees on the front!"

Elle and Laurette stood in the gym wearing cheerleading uniforms stitched together from old ballet costumes. The blasé, skeptical Beverly Hills squad sat on the bleachers in front of them. Elle was waiting for Savannah to arrive so she could show off Bibi's cheerleading routine. She had recruited Laurette to practice with her in her backyard the night before. When it got dark, Bernard had turned on the floodlights and they had worked until they had it down pretty well, considering the fact that neither one of them had ever been a cheerleader.

"I love that about you, Elle," Chessie said. "The way your inner child is so, like, totally outer."

"Your inner child is showing, too, Chessie," Laurette said. "I can see it now—it looks just like a baby vampire bat."

"Laurette, that was mean," Elle said.

Savannah swept in, looking fresh and sexy in white shorts and a matching tank. "I'm sorry, Elle," Savannah said. "The team took a vote and decided we don't need any help."

"What?" Elle couldn't believe it. They weren't even giving her a chance to show them how she could help? They were dismissing her just like that?

"How can you say you don't need help?" Laurette said. "You guys couldn't get any worse!"

"Hey!" Jenna cried. She lunged at Laurette as if she might hit her, but Chloe and Rachel held her back. "We work hard!"

"Sure," Laurette said. "On your tans."

"Elle, I just wanted you to know, *I* voted for you," Chessie said loud enough for Elle, Laurette, and Savannah to hear. "But the other girls think you're kind of a loser. I told them you just look like a loser, you're really not one at all, and anyway, you shouldn't judge people just because they have no style—"

"Gee, thanks, Chessie," Elle said. She wasn't going to let these girls get rid of her so easily, not after all the preparation she'd done.

"I've got a hot new routine to show you," Elle said. "We're all here now. Why don't you let me and Laurette do the routine? It will only take a minute. If you don't like it, we'll leave. And I'll never bring this up again."

"Yeah, and you can go back to entertaining your three fans," Laurette said.

Savannah looked at her teammates for approval.

"We already voted," Chessie said. "What's the point?"

"Is this going to make practice go late?" Jenna asked. "I want to get to the Gucci store before it closes. If I don't buy their new bag today, I'll have to kill myself."

"Your bag can wait," Savannah said. "I think we

should give Elle a chance. And I don't care what the rest of you think. I'm the captain, and I say, everybody, shut up and watch."

"Thanks, Savannah!" Elle pressed PLAY on the portable CD player she'd brought, and funky music filled the gym.

"Ready? Let's go!" Elle and Laurette danced, jumped, and kicked while chanting the cheer Bibi had taught her, substituting "Beverly" for "Armadillo." At the end, Laurette even tossed Elle into the air. Elle perched on Laurette's shoulder, arms out in a V for "victory." She checked the cheerleaders for their reaction.

They stared at her with their mouths open, amazed. But was it good amazed or bad amazed? Elle hopped down off Laurette's shoulder.

"I was thinking at the end, since there are ten of you, instead of a shoulder-sit you could do a tri-hitch pyramid, and then the fliers can do spread-eagle dismounts while the bases crumble and roll," Elle said.

"What?" Jenna asked. "What are you talking about?"

"You don't know what a tri-hitch is?" Elle said. "Hmmm. Well, I can't do one by myself—you need at least three people. But I could draw it for you."

"I don't know," Chloe said. "That routine looked hard. It, like, reeked of *effort*."

"I don't like to look like I'm trying too hard, ever," Rachel said.

"If we do that we might get sweaty!" Jenna said. "And I look like the Bride of Chucky when my makeup runs."

"It's not as hard as it looks," Elle said. "If I can do it, you guys can definitely do it. I mean, I'm not even a cheerleader! And look at you—you guys are practically pros!"

Chessie glanced at Savannah, who said nothing, but was watching Elle intently. "Admit it, Elle," Chessie said. "You're making these stunt names up."

"No, they're real!" Elle said. "This friend of mine was a cheerleader in Texas—the cheerleading capital of the galaxy!—and she showed me all these cool tricks—"

"What friend is that?" Chessie asked. "Why doesn't she come show us these tricks herself?"

"Well, because she's working," Elle said. "She's a manicurist."

"A manicurist?" Chloe said. "You're teaching us stuff you learned at a nail salon?"

"Where else would I have picked up so much

information?" Elle said. "You can learn just about anything at a nail salon. Anyway, she really knows her cheerleading."

"You're so crazy, Elle!" Chessie chirped. "Really, it's adorable. Thanks for showing us your little dance, but we've got work to do now, right, Savannah? Okay, go! Scoot! Nice manicure, by the way."

The other girls were frowning.

Elle couldn't believe her routine hadn't won them over. She stooped to pick up her CD case.

"I liked it," Savannah said.

Everyone stopped speaking. Elle turned around to look at Savannah.

"I want to do it," Savannah continued. "Girls, we're going to learn that routine today. We're going to know it cold by Friday's game."

"Really?" Elle glanced at Laurette, who grinned and gave her a thumbs-up.

"I don't care who voted for what," Savannah said. "Elle, you're hired."

"All right!" Elle squealed.

"Congratulations, Elle!" Chessie said, coming over to pat her on the back. "I knew you could do it! I was rooting for you all along!"

"Do you need me anymore, Elle?" Laurette asked.

"I'm finding it a little hard to breathe in here. Too much hot air."

"Thanks for your help," Elle said. "I couldn't have done it without you."

"Lucky you, now you get to spend even more time with these lovely human beings," Laurette said. "If you can turn them into a good squad, I owe you a veggie burger."

"Deal," Elle said.

Laurette left, and Savannah ordered the squad to line up.

"Okay," Elle said. "Let's try a pyramid first. That's pretty basic. We need to assign everyone a position. Rachel, Chloe, Jenna, and Tori—you're the biggest, so you be bases." She pointed out the four tallest, strongest-looking girls.

"I'm going on the Cheese-and-Pickle Diet," Jenna said, "so in a few weeks I'm going to be a lot smaller."

"You don't need to go on a diet," Elle said. "But for now, you four get on your hands and knees."

"Ick, it's all dirty down there," Chloe complained.

"Just do what Elle says," Savannah said.

"All right," Elle said. "Emma, Caitlin, and Malia, you be the second level." The three girls hesitated. "Go ahead, get on top of them."

"Don't break our backs," Rachel said.

"They're just as heavy as we are," Jenna said.

Elle ignored the griping. "Now, Savannah and Chessie will be the torches. You stand on the side of the pyramid doing the Liberty. And you help spot P.J., who will be the flier."

She positioned Savannah and Chessie on the side of the pyramid, on the backs of Jenna and Chloe. P.J. climbed up to stand on top of the second row of girls.

"Now, P.J., can you do a Liberty?" Elle showed P.J. a move she'd just learned herself. Standing on one leg, she lifted the other straight behind her and held up her arms as if she were holding the torch of the Statue of Liberty. P.J., the smallest and most limber member of the squad, got it right away.

"Good. Wow, if only you guys could see how great this looks. Okay, Chessie and Savannah, you both do a scale." Elle demonstrated the pose, balancing on one leg with the other out to the side. "Then you spot P.J. while she jumps off the pyramid in a high front hurdler." Elle showed a flying leap with one leg out in front, as if she were jumping over a hurdle in track. "Got it?"

Savannah lifted her leg up straight in front of her, but Chessie was having trouble. "Lift your leg higher, Chessie," Elle said. Chessie kicked her leg up, lost her balance, and knocked P.J. to the floor. The equilibrium of the pyramid was ruined. The girls tumbled down, one layer on top of the other, groaning.

"Ow! Is this supposed to hurt?" Tori cried.

"Chessie! What are you doing? You ruined the whole thing!" Rachel said.

"I did not," Chessie said. "Elle pushed me!"

"Hmmm," Elle said. Chessie was obviously talent-challenged. "Let's make a change. Chessie, you be a base, and Malia, you be a torch."

"What?" Chessie cried. "But she's taller than I am!"

"Chessie, get on your hands and knees," Savannah said. "Now."

"Come to think of it," Elle said. "Maybe you'd better take a spot on the bottom row."

Chessie threw her a dirty look, but did as she was told. "I'll do anything for the squad," she said. "I just think maybe Elle, since she just learned all this yesterday from a manicurist, might not know what she's talking about."

It was true that Elle was a beginner. She was faking her way through this, bolstered by the confidence and the information Bibi had given her. But Elle's sharp eye—the same eye that knew just how many rhinestones should decorate a T-shirt, or just what shade of red paint would result in the perfect Valentine's Day heart—carried her through. The more she bossed these cheerleaders around, the more sure of herself she felt. She even began to improve on standard formations and invent new ones that looked better to her. The cheerleaders picked up on her confidence—all except Chessie, who stumbled with every move.

The problem, according to Chessie, was that Elle's moves weren't challenging enough. "We're so beyond all this," she said. "It's throwing me off my game."

At the end of practice Savannah said, "Okay, that's enough. Good work today, you guys."

While the other girls hit the showers, Savannah approached Elle. Chessie tagged along.

"Thanks, Elle—this new routine will really help us," Savannah said. "You know, it's buried kind of deep, but you've got a sense of style."

"She does have a style all her own," Chessie said. "Like, who else could pull off those thick glasses?"

"Thanks," Elle said.

"So listen, my friend Amber's having a big party this Saturday," Savannah said. "Why don't you come? It will be fun."

Elle felt the fine blonde hairs on her forearms bristle with excitement. Go to a party? That Saturday? With Savannah and her friends? Would Hunter be there? Elle was afraid to ask. But the chances were good. In fact, the chances were excellent. Maybe she'd finally get to talk to him, make him notice her. This was her big opportunity!

"Elle's too busy," Chessie said. "She's learning all these cheers to teach us, and she probably can't come. Right, Elle?"

"I'd love to come," Elle said. "Can I bring Laurette?"

"Who's Laurette?" Savannah asked.

"You know, my friend who did the routine with me today," Elle said.

"I can see why you wouldn't notice her, Savannah," Chessie said. "She kind of flies under your radar. Like Elle. That's why they're friends. Because they're the same type—not particularly noticeable. Not offensive or anything—"

"Sure, whatever," Savannah said. Then she turned to face Elle. "The party's in Malibu. Amber's dad has a beach house."

Elle could hardly contain her excitement. "Great! I'll be there."

"I'll be there, too," Chessie said. "It's so cool of you to invite me, Savannah."

"I didn't," Savannah said. "But you can come if you feel the need."

Chessie laughed. "If I feel the need. You're so funny, Savannah. I love the way you kid around with me. You always tease your favorites, right? It's like a sign of friendship, right? I can tell you mean it in a totally friendly way—"

Savannah turned on her heel and walked away in the middle of Chessie's sentence. Chessie started to trot after her, then thought better of it and stopped.

"Wow! A beach party! I can't wait!" Elle said. "Savannah's so nice. I never would have thought someone so popular and so beautiful would be so friendly. But I guess she really is as perfect as she seems."

"She's too nice, really," Chessie said. "I think she just invited you to Amber's party because she didn't want to hurt your feelings. I mean, she was inviting me, but you were standing here drooling all over her like a lapdog, and what choice did she have? She had to invite you."

"What—?" Elle didn't believe it.

"I wouldn't go if I were you," Chessie said. "She

was sweet to ask you, but you'd probably have a terrible time. You know, feeling all left out and like you don't fit in . . . I'd hate to see your self-esteem take such a beating."

"Don't worry about my self-esteem," Elle said. "It can take it."

Chapter 8

"ELLE, WHAT'S the matter?" It was seven o'clock on Saturday evening, and Laurette had come over to Elle's house early so they could get ready for the party together. She had found Elle sitting on the floor of her room, cross-legged, staring at the open closet.

"I'm paralyzed," Elle said.

"What?" Laurette cried, running to Elle and pulling her to her feet. Elle managed to stand and scratch her nose.

"You're not paralyzed," Laurette said.

"Not literally," Elle said. "I'm paralyzed with fear and uncertainty."

"Oh," Laurette said. "Welcome to my world."

"Hunter is probably going to be at Amber's party," Elle said. "I need to make him notice me soon. I only have two months until Prom. If he's going to be my date, he's going to have to start realizing I'm alive."

"For sure," Laurette said.

"So, what I wear tonight could determine my entire future," Elle said. "I've never given my clothes so much thought before. It's overwhelming! They have so much power! I can't take it!" Panicking, she threw herself on the bed and hid her face in the blankets. How would she ever choose something to wear for her first true encounter with Hunter, the future love of her life? What outfit could possibly be good enough?

"Elle, calm down," Laurette said. "It's not that big a deal. Maybe Hunter won't even notice what you're wearing."

"But that's just it," Elle said. "I need him to notice me. He has to notice something about me, and so far, my face, my figure, and my sparkling personality don't seem to have done the trick."

"You've got tons of clothes." Laurette went to the closet and started sliding the hangers across the racks. "I've never seen most of these. Have you ever worn them?"

"No, but I've rearranged them by color and length several times to form lots of pretty patterns."

"Hmmm," Laurette said. "Well, the best way to get noticed is to be flashy. That's what my mom does. She likes to be stunning—literally. She says if the room doesn't fall silent when she walks in, she's not dressed up enough." Laurette's mother, Margarita, had once been a Las Vegas showgirl. Her idea of modest dress was anything without beads.

"It's true," Elle said. "My mother always says your mother would stand out in a crowd of flamingos." She pulled a bright orange dress out of the closet and waved it at Laurette. It had cutouts at the sides and was made of a fabric meant to cling in all the right places. "What about this? This dress says, 'Go ahead. Try to ignore me.'"

"Try it on," Laurette said.

Elle tried on the dress. It felt a little tight.

"Wow," Laurette said. "It looks like it was made for you."

"I think that it needs a little something else," Elle said as she gazed at her reflection in the mirror. "How about a scarf belt around the hips?" She turned and noticed Laurette's expression. Then she added shyly, "I saw that in a magazine last week."

Laurette watched as her friend expertly wrapped

the floral scarf over her hips. "That looks fantastic!" Laurette exclaimed.

"Now for some jewelry." Elle rummaged through her jewelry case until she came across a pair of chandelier earrings. She held them up against the dress. "That really says *ka-pow*!"

"I can't believe that you just pulled that whole outfit together!" Laurette said in awe.

"And what about these glasses?" Elle picked up a pair of glasses from her dresser. She had glued multicolored rhinestones on them, just for fun. "Funky, huh?" Elle put on the glittery glasses. "How do I look?"

"Hot!" Laurette said. "If Hunter doesn't notice that outfit, he's color-blind. Or just plain blind."

"Maybe you're right," Elle said. "I need to be bold. Really put myself out there. Say, 'Here I am!'"

"Yeah!" Laurette said. "Be hot stuff. Like one of those dancers in a rap video."

With a few finishing touches Elle was ready. Laurette threw on a fun vintage dress, and they were all set.

"Elle, where are you two going dressed like that?" her mother asked, peering into her room a few minutes later. She beamed with pride as she looked at Elle.

"What do you think?" Elle asked.

"You look absolutely stunning," Eva said with a huge smile on her face.

"Come on, Elle. Let's roll," Laurette said.

Without another word, the pair headed out, ready for the party . . . and perhaps for Elle's date with Mr. Right.

Elle and Laurette parked along the side of the road—the driveway was full—and walked up to Amber's beach house. Music blasted from the windows, and Elle could already hear giggly, hoarse voices indicating a party in full swing. "Wow, sounds like a fun party," Elle said.

"We'll see," Laurette said. She rang the doorbell. A tall, haughty girl with long black hair answered. Elle didn't know her.

"Amber, did you hire some kind of freaky-deaky DJs to play at your party?" the girl yelled over her shoulder into the house.

"This is not a good sign," Laurette whispered to Elle.

"She's just joking," Elle said. "Maybe it's her way of being friendly."

Amber, aptly named with her shiny, copper-colored hair, appeared at the door in a plaid bikini.

"No, Marissa," she said. "I didn't hire anyone. Who are you?" she asked Elle and Laurette.

"We're friends of Savannah Shaw," Elle said. "She invited us to your party. I hope it's okay."

Amber looked confused. "You are? You're friends of Savannah's?"

"That's what we said," Laurette said. "Are you going to let us in or not?"

"Well—I guess so," Amber said. "Come on in. Everyone's out back."

Elle and Laurette followed Amber and Marissa through the house. Kids were hanging out in the den, in the kitchen, and on a large back terrace that overlooked the ocean. Everybody was dressed casually in jeans, sundresses, or swimsuit cover-ups.

Elle felt way overdressed, but she put it out of her mind. She was here now, and the important thing was to have fun and make an impression on Hunter. At least she'd stand out in the crowd. She kept an eye out for Hunter, but she didn't see him.

"Elle! Wow, you showed up." Chessie, dressed in jeans and a halter top, was grooving on the terrace with Rachel and Chloe; they all held drinks in their hands. "That took guts."

"Thank you," Elle said. "I was a little nervous about coming. I'm glad you're here! I was afraid I wouldn't know anyone. I had the hardest time deciding what to wear."

"I can see that," Chessie said. "And I see you brought your Raggedy Ann doll with you."

"You know, in cool places, vintage is the height of chic," Laurette snapped.

"Oh, I'm sure," Chessie said. "Cool places like the wax museum."

Elle caught Chloe elbowing Chessie. Chessie looked toward the door. Elle turned to see what they were looking at.

And there he was, gleaming and scrumptious in pale-green polo shirt and jeans, his black hair shining in the light from the tiki lanterns that burned around the terrace. Hunter had arrived.

Elle's heart seemed to plummet to the pit of her stomach. She felt all goofy and nervous. He made her speechless.

"I love this song," Chessie said as the latest hip-hop hit blared from the stereo speakers. "Let's dance." She said it very specifically to Chloe and Rachel, excluding Elle and Laurette. Chessie and her friends moved to an open spot on the terrace and started dancing in a slithery, sexy way. Or they tried to, anyway. Chloe and Rachel were good dancers, but Chessie kept jerking her head back as if she were having a seizure. Obviously, they were trying to show off for Hunter.

Elle watched him. He glanced briefly at the dancing girls, then went back inside the house.

"Let's go inside," Elle said to Laurette.

"Yes, let's," Laurette said. "Chessie's dancing is giving me motion sickness."

Savannah stepped through the sliding glass door just as they were about to go inside. Her skin was tan and glowing. She wore a bikini top and a short sarong skirt, and her feet were bare.

"Elle, you made it," she said, ignoring Laurette. "Um, you're all dressed up. Didn't I tell you this was a casual party?"

Elle's glasses suddenly slid halfway down her nose. She pushed them back into place. "I thought I'd dress up."

"Dress up? Well, you definitely did that," Savannah said.

Chessie spotted Savannah and ran over to her. "Savannah! Thank God you're here. I thought I was going to die of boredom, but now that you're here the party can get started for real. I love what you're wearing." Chessie slipped off her sandals as she talked. "Look—I'm barefoot, too!"

"Can you move over, Chessie?" Savannah said. "I was talking to Elle."

Chessie pouted and stepped aside. "Don't you just *love* what Elle's wearing?" she said to Savannah.

"I couldn't pull off wearing that," Savannah said, "but Elle's so cute and original, she does pull it off. Now I feel underdressed!" She flipped her hair and looked right at Elle. "Come with me, I'll get you something to drink." She put her arm around Elle's shoulders, dragging her away from Chessie and Laurette, who were left to follow behind. Savannah was acting as if Laurette were invisible. Elle glanced back at her friend to make sure she was okay, and Laurette gave her a sarcastic little wave.

"What would you like? Beer? Wine?" Savannah asked, leading Elle into the kitchen.

"Thanks, I'll have a beer," Chessie said.

"Not you," Savannah said. "Do me a favor, Chess? Find out if Bryce is here yet."

Bryce was the cute lacrosse player Savannah had a crush on. "I haven't seen him," Chessie said.

"So, go look," Savannah said.

"Okay. Be right back," Chessie said.

"So, Elle, what would you like?" Savannah asked.

"I'll have a ginger ale," Elle said.

"You got it. Amber, could you fix Elle a ginger ale?"

Amber stood by the refrigerator, talking to Hunter and a blond surfer dude. She glanced dismissively at Savannah. "Can't she get it herself?"

"Sure I can," Elle said. "I—"

"I just thought, since you're the hostess—" Savannah said.

Amber rolled her eyes and continued talking to Hunter and the surfer. But she stepped slightly away from the fridge, as a concession to Savannah. Elle opened the door, reached in, and grabbed a soda.

"Do you want anything, Laurette?" Elle asked, turning around. But Laurette had disappeared. Huh, Elle thought. Maybe she went to the bathroom.

"Elle, I want to talk cheerleading with you for a minute," Savannah said. She led Elle to a couch in the living room, where two girls were already sitting. "Move," she said to the girls, waving them away. The girls looked up, defiantly at first. But the sight of Savannah intimidated them, and they scurried away like mice.

Savannah sat down. "I really love your ideas," she said. "The new moves rock. But what about our uniforms? Do you think they're hot enough? I was looking at the Speedsters' outfits last week, and they were so much sexier than ours. Belly shirts, and that red vinyl . . . We looked like nuns next to them."

"You do need new outfits," Elle said. "We'll have to think of a way to raise money to buy some. The best ones aren't cheap."

"You'll come up with something, won't you?" Savannah said. "You're so good at this."

"Sure, I'll think about it," Elle said. "It shouldn't be hard to raise money in Beverly Hills. Everybody's got plenty."

"Yeah, but nobody cares about the basketball team, or the cheerleaders," Savannah said. "That's the problem, getting their attention. And getting them to care."

Just then, Savannah spotted her lacrosse player. "There's Bryce," Savannah said. "Why didn't Chessie tell me he was here?" Elle noticed he'd brought a lacrosse stick to the party. That seemed typical of Bryce.

He must feel insecure, Elle thought. That lacrosse stick is his security blanket.

"I've got to zero in on him before Marissa digs her claws in too deep," Savannah said.

"He'd never choose Marissa over you," Elle said. "You're so much prettier. You're the prettiest girl here. The prettiest girl at the whole school."

"I know, but believe it or not, some guys like to play the field. They like to act all hard to get and make girls crazy. I know I'll get Bryce eventually, but he's making me play the game. So, here goes. Have fun."

Elle took a widemouthed plastic cup from a stack on the kitchen counter. She dropped some ice in it and poured in her ginger ale. Where was Laurette? Where was Hunter? She walked out of the kitchen, keeping an eye out for both of them.

She found Hunter in the den, sitting on a sofa surrounded by girls, including Chessie.

"You made a free throw in the last game that was a thing of beauty," Chessie was saying. "You're always making great shots. Of course, I see every game. Not like most people I know." She looked meaningfully at the girls around her, who weren't cheerleaders and didn't go to many basketball games.

"Thanks," Hunter said. "But we still lost the game. By about a zillion points."

"You're too modest," Chessie said. "I mean, sure you lost the game. We lose every game. But you're still a great player."

"Are you going to play basketball in college, Hunter?" another girl asked.

"Probably," Hunter said. "I'm waiting to see where I'm accepted."

"I bet you get a scholarship," the girl said.

"I don't know," Hunter said. "Not many college scouts visit Beverly Hills High looking for prospects."

"Maybe my mom could help you," Chessie said. "Did you know she's an accountant for the Lakers?"

"No, I didn't know that," Hunter said. "But—"

"She probably knows somebody who knows somebody who could help you," Chessie said. "She's always pulling strings for people."

Hunter stood up. "That's okay. I'll be right back."

He left the circle of girls beaming up at him and headed for the bathroom.

Now's my chance, Elle thought. If I can catch him coming out of the bathroom, I can be alone with him for at least a few seconds, before the swarm figures out where he is.

She positioned herself outside the bathroom door, as if she were waiting to use it herself. "There's another bathroom upstairs," Amber said as she walked by.

"That's all right, I'll wait for this one," Elle said.

A few minutes later the bathroom door opened. Elle blocked it. Hunter looked down at her and blinked.

"Excuse me," he said.

"Oh—sorry!" Elle stepped aside, blocking the hallway and his path back to the den.

"Um—I'm going that way," he said.

"Oh, me, too," Elle said, but she didn't move. She gripped her drink in her sweaty hand. Her glasses slipped down her nose. She pushed them back up again without thinking about it.

"So . . . maybe we should start walking in that direction," Hunter said. "I don't want to be rude, but—"

Elle pretended to laugh. "Oh! Right. Silly me. Ha-ha." She leaned against the wall. "You know, your speech at that pep rally last Friday really got to me."

"It did?"

Elle could feel her glasses slipping down her nose again. She'd have to get them fixed. "Beverly Hills is such a great school, you know?" she said. "But the students don't appreciate it. There's no school spirit. I thought that was what you were really saying when you asked people to come to the basketball games."

"You're right," Hunter said. "You're totally right. Beverly Hills could be so much better. People could care about each other more. Like my teammates, some of them are good players, but they just don't try. School spirit doesn't mean anything to them. All they care about is chicks and partying."

"You know what, Hunter?" Elle said.

But Chessie interrupted her. "There you are," Chessie said to Hunter. She leaned toward Elle and sniffed. Then she waved her hand in front of her nose as if something smelled bad. "Oh, Elle, do you want a breath mint?" She pulled a tin of extra-strong mints out of her bag.

Elle's hand flew to her mouth. Did she have bad breath? Had Hunter noticed? She took one of Chessie's mints and thanked her. Better safe than sorry.

"Want to go for a walk on the beach with me, Hunter?" Chessie asked.

"Uh, maybe in a minute," Hunter said, but Chessie yanked on his arm and accidentally knocked Elle's cup. A little ginger ale splashed out onto her dress. Elle looked down to inspect the damage, and her glasses slid right down her nose. They plopped into her cup, splattering Hunter, Chessie, and herself with soda.

"I'm sorry!" she cried.

"Elle, your glasses!" Chessie said. She reached into Elle's cup and dug them out with her fingers.

"They're all wet and sticky. I hope they'll be all right. They're so special-looking, too, with all those diamonds all over them. Or rhinestones, right? They're not real diamonds—no, they wouldn't be. You'd better go rinse them off. Can you see okay without them? Do you need someone to lead you to the sink? Oh, there's the bathroom, right there. You can make it by yourself, can't you?"

Elle had no choice but to go to the sink while Chessie dragged Hunter away, clucking, "Poor Elle—she's such a klutz!"

Elle, her vision hazy without her glasses, retreated into the bathroom, mortified.

Hunter must think I'm an idiot, she thought. A blind idiot with bad breath. I made an impression, all right—a bad impression. That's it, she decided. Zosia is right. The glasses have to go.

Chapter 9

ELLE WASHED and dried her glasses. All she wanted now was to see a friendly face, and Laurette had the friendliest face she knew.

She searched the house, but there was no sign of Laurette. From the terrace she noticed a bonfire on the beach, and she went down the rickety wooden stairs to see who was there.

A subset of the party had gathered around the bonfire. Laurette was sitting on a log, talking to a brown-haired boy wearing a battered T-shirt that read: I'M CHEVY CHASE AND YOU'RE NOT.

"There you are," Elle said to Laurette. "I was looking for you."

"I figured Savannah was taking good care of

you," Laurette said. "I didn't exactly feel welcome up there. So I came down here to look at the ocean, and Darren and I started talking—"

The boy looked up at Elle and said, "That would be me."

"I'm Elle."

The boy looked familiar—she'd seen him at school. He was thin and almost as pale as Elle herself.

"I like your glasses," he said. "You look like Elton John." He made it sound like a good thing, which was nice for a change.

"Thanks," Elle said. "You ready to go soon, Laurette? I think I've humiliated myself enough for one night."

Laurette got to her feet. "What happened?"

"I'll tell you in the car," Elle said.

Darren stood up, too. "Hey—I'll see you at school."

"Cool," Laurette said. "See you at school."

She and Elle trudged up the steps and around the house to find Elle's car. "He seems nice," Elle said.

"He's a senior and he plays guitar in a band called Warp Factor Five," Laurette said. "Isn't he cute? We talked for almost an hour. But he didn't ask me out or anything."

"Maybe he will when he sees you at school," Elle said.

"I kept giving him openings, but he didn't take them. I mentioned a band I want to see tomorrow night, thinking he might want to go, too. He didn't say anything."

"You just met him," Elle said.

"I know," Laurette said. "But I really like him! Elle, remember last week when Hunter gave that speech at the pep rally and you suddenly knew you were in love with him? I think that's happening to me. I think Darren is my Hunter."

"Wow, Laurette, that's huge." Laurette had mentioned boys she liked to Elle before, but not like this. "That's super huge. I'm so happy for you!"

"Well, I have to get him to like me first," Laurette said. "Or there won't be anything to be happy about. Just pain and misery."

"I know what you mean," Elle said. She felt a pang as she glanced back up at the house. Through the window she could see Chessie throwing her head back to laugh at something Hunter had said. Of course he'd like Chessie more—she was a cheerleader, she was popular, she knew what to wear and how to act at parties. And she didn't have bad breath.

"Laurette, how's my breath?" Elle breathed in her direction.

"Not bad," Laurette said. "A slight hint of ginger ale and mint. Why?"

"I had bad breath before, but Chessie gave me a mint and saved me."

"I'll bet she did," Laurette said, rolling her eyes.

"You have made the right decision," Zosia said. Elle sat at the vanity table in her mother's room while Zosia stood behind her, supervising the insertion of Elle's first pair of contact lenses. "We'll start you out with regular plain lenses, since your eyes are such a lovely, natural, bright blue. Here are your drops. This is my own special organic formula. The key is to keep your eyes nice and moist—Don't let them get dry. Okay?"

"Okay." Elle balanced the tiny, delicate lens on her fingertip. She couldn't believe it was really going to go into her eye.

"Don't be shy. Just pop it right in."

She guided Elle's hand as Elle put in one lens, then the other. Elle blinked at her image in the mirror. Zosia gasped.

"Oh, Ellie. I can see your whole face, no clunky

glasses hiding you. You look so beautiful! This is going to change your life, you'll see."

Elle's eyes adjusted to the lenses. The contacts didn't bother her at all, now that she was getting used to them. She had never been able to see herself without glasses before—because without her glasses on, she couldn't see. She had large, clear, blue eyes with long, pale eyelashes. She really did look much better.

I've been hiding behind those glasses all along, she realized. Now there's no hiding. Just me, my face, out there in the world. Take it or leave it.

"Zosia, you're a miracle worker!" Eva came into the room and applauded Elle's new look. "How did you get her to do it?"

"All it took was a little embarrassment," Zosia said. "That always does the trick."

Eva threw her arms around Elle. "Darling, isn't that so much better? I can't stop looking at you! Wait until your father sees you!"

Elle instinctively reached up to slide her nonexistent glasses up her nose. Zosia lightly slapped her hand.

"Get that hand away from your face! That's a bad habit you're going to have to get rid of quick."

"Zosia's right, darling," Eva said. "You shouldn't

touch your face—it causes pimples, and it can smudge your makeup."

"I don't wear makeup," Elle said.

"I keep forgetting," Eva said. "What kind of girl doesn't wear makeup? Well, maybe now you'll start."

"Yes," Zosia said. "A little shadow to bring out the blue in your eyes, a little mascara for those pale lashes—"

"Hold on," Elle said. "Just because I'm wearing contact lenses, that doesn't mean I'll change myself from head to toe. It's just a tiny adjustment. I'm still the same."

"Whatever you say, dear," Eva said, winking at Zosia.

"I saw that!" Elle said.

"Look at you!" Bibi said when Elle returned to Pamperella for her manicure. Elle's nails still looked great from the previous visit, but she needed to talk to someone, and there was no one better than Bibi. "No more braces, no more glasses! You're becoming a real glamour girl!"

"Do you think so?" Elle asked. She wasn't sure how she felt about becoming a glamour girl. When she looked in the mirror, she saw the same old mousy Elle. Maybe without glasses or braces, but still—no glamour girl.

"How did the cheerleaders like that routine I showed you?" Bibi asked. "Did it go over well?"

"It took a little convincing, but luckily, Savannah is on my side," Elle said. "The others pretty much have to do whatever she wants. She's the queen and the head cheerleader."

"Good for you," Bibi said. "It's always good to stay on the right side of those queen bee types. Now, listen, I'll show you some more flashy moves later. But the next thing those girls need are some new uniforms. Something with a little kick to them. You know, sexy. If the girls look sexy enough, they won't have to be that good—people will still want to come see them."

"And if they come to see the cheerleaders, they have to sit through the basketball games, too," Elle said.

"Right. No matter how miserable. But it is better if the cheerleaders are actually good. And it's really better if the basketball team wins once in a while. You can only go so far without a win. People need that satisfaction. But one step at a time. You'll get there, Elle. I know it. You can do anything you set your mind to."

Elle had brought a cheerleading-supply catalog, and she and Bibi pored over it. Bibi pointed out the outfits she thought would be most effective.

"Stay away from any pastel colors," she recommended. "They're death on most complexions, especially the blonde type common to the Beverly Hills princess. Stick with strong, clean, bold colors. What are your school colors, anyway?"

"Blue and gold," Elle said.

"Good, those are classic," Bibi said. "What's your mascot?"

"Officially, it's the bluefin tuna," Elle said.

Bibi wrinkled her nose. "You people . . . jeez, the things you don't know about high-school sports. Bluefin tuna! How could you get it so wrong?"

"I know," Elle said. "I'm working on changing it to the Killer Bees."

"Smart girl," Bibi said. "Bees are great! You can do all kinds of cool cheers with that buzzing sound." Then, referring to Elle's contact lenses, she asked, "So what prompted the big change?"

"I was at a party last night, talking to Hunter," Elle began.

"He's that basketball boy you like?" Bibi said.

Elle nodded. "And my glasses slipped off my nose and fell into my drink. I got ginger ale all over his shirt. It was so embarrassing. I finally get a chance to talk to him, and I totally blow it."

"That's not so bad," Bibi said. "Now he'll remember you."

"Yeah, as a dork."

"No, no. This is just the kind of cute story people tell after they get together! Maybe he thought it was funny."

"I doubt it. Everyone kept telling me I looked like Elton John."

"Hmmm . . . well, that's not normally a good look for a girl. But maybe you made it work."

"Trust me, I didn't. That's why I got rid of the glasses."

"Well, I think you were right to do it," Bibi said. "You look great. I think I'll paint your nails a slightly redder shade of pink today, if you don't object. Something bolder, for the bold new Elle. What do you think?"

"I'll take any help I can get—even help from nail polish," Elle said.

"Elle! You lost your glasses!" Chessie said when Elle saw her on Monday morning. "You poor thing! You must be blind as a bat. Here, let me guide you to your locker." She took Elle's arm and led her down the hall.

"That's okay, Chessie," Elle said. "I can see. Really."

Chessie blinked. "You can? That's wonderful!" She held up three fingers and said, "How many fingers am I holding up?"

"Three," Elle said.

"Wow, what happened?" Chessie said. "Was it some kind of miracle, like when a saint appears in a water stain on somebody's ceiling? Did you go to a faith healer? This is amazing!"

"No, I just got contacts," Elle said.

"But I thought you were allergic to them or something," Chessie said. "I always say thank God I don't have to wear contacts. Because some of the stories I've heard . . . Did you know one of my cousins actually went blind from wearing contacts? The lens fused itself with her eyeball. They had to do an operation to fix it, but she can't go out during daylight hours. I hope nothing like that happens to you."

Elle was horrified. "I hope not, too! That's just the kind of thing I was afraid of. That's why I wouldn't give up my glasses all those years."

"That was smart," Chessie said. "If I were you I'd switch back to glasses. Maybe not the ones you were wearing at the party. I didn't want to say it then, but they were pretty dorky. But contacts can turn you into a crusty-eyed freak."

"I'm sure that doesn't happen very often," Laurette interjected. She'd been standing nearby and had overheard a lot of the conversation.

"It doesn't matter how often it happens," Chessie said. "If it happens just once to *you*, you're wrecked for life. I'm glad I don't have to worry about it. You wouldn't catch me dead in glasses— *ick*. Luckily I have perfect twenty-twenty vision."

"I wish I did." Elle's hand instinctively flew to her face. Her poor eyes! They felt okay for now, but what if something terrible happened?

"When you have a perfectly oval face like mine, glasses throw off the whole balance of your features," Chessie said.

"Don't you have some glass to chew on, Chessie?" Laurette said, pulling Elle away. "Don't listen to her," she said to Elle. "She'll just get you all upset over nothing."

"But what if she's right?" Elle said. "Now I know to watch for danger signs of my eyes crusting over."

"Yeah. Right." Laurette studied Elle's face. "You look really pretty without your glasses, Elle. I think Chessie's just jealous of you."

"Jealous of me? How could someone as cool as Chessie be jealous of me?"

Laurette shrugged. "Weirder things have happened." She glanced at Elle's hands now. "Did you get another manicure?"

Elle proudly flashed her hand. "It's Ripcord Red. Isn't it a beautiful color? I love the way my nails shine now, too."

"No glasses, no braces, and a perfect manicure . . ." Laurette said. "What's happening to the dowdy Elle I know and love? You're changing."

"No, I'm not," Elle insisted. "Sure, maybe a few little things are changing on the outside. But inside I'm still the same me."

"I hope you stay that way," Laurette said. "I love the same old you."

"I love the same old you, too," Elle said. "Let's promise never to change."

"Promise."

Chapter 10

"THE NEW uniforms are here!" Elle cried on Thursday afternoon. She dropped a big box on the gym floor.

It had been easy for Elle to get the money for the new uniforms. The PTA president had been a cheerleader in high school, and after Elle's appeal for new uniforms she quickly wrote a check.

All the cheerleaders were practicing the new routines, and Elle was impressed. They'd improved a lot already, and it had been only a couple of weeks.

The squad gathered around as Elle tore open the box. "Finally," Chloe said. "They'd better be good."

Elle pulled out a plastic bag and ripped it open. She held up the new top and skirt. The top was sleeveless, royal blue, and cropped at the waist. It had simple, shiny, gold trim and the new Killer Bees logo Elle had designed, in glowing golden letters. The skirt was short, pleated, and all gold, with matching gold panties.

"What do you think?" Elle asked.

"Wow," Chloe said. "Those are hot!"

"The other teams will be blinded by all that gold," Jenna said.

"They totally rock," Savannah said.

"Good job, Elle," Chessie said. "You're very good at flipping through a catalog and ordering something. Who knew you could handle the pressure?"

"Let's go try them on," Savannah said, giving Chessie a nasty glare. The girls retreated to the locker room. When they returned, they looked stunning. Elle watched them practice their routines. They stayed together, showing good form, and shouted out their cheers proudly. It was almost as if the fabulous new outfits motivated them to do better.

I never realized clothes had so much power, Elle thought. But they really do. They can change your mood, the way you feel about yourself, the way you behave . . . it's almost like magic.

"Savannah, I think you should hold another pep rally tomorrow afternoon," Elle said. "Show the other kids your new uniforms and a preview of your new tricks, and get them talking about the Killer Bees. Maybe we'll get more people to show up at the game tomorrow night."

"Good thinking, Elle," Savannah said. "Or better yet—what if the girls wore their new uniforms all day long tomorrow? To really get people talking."

"Go for it," Elle said.

The students attending Friday's pep rally were still fairly apathetic, but when the cheerleaders appeared in their golden outfits and pulled off a couple of impressive new stunts, the students reacted.

"Wow," Elle overheard one boy saying to another. "I never realized the cheerleaders were so hot. . . ."

"I know," his friend said. "Let's stop by the game tonight. We don't have to stay if it sucks. But I wouldn't mind checking out more of Savannah Shaw's moves."

It's working! Elle said to herself. My plan is slowly working!

♥   ♥   ♥

"Wow, Elle," Laurette said that night at the game—the Beverly Hills Killer Bees versus the Venice Vultures. "The cheerleaders don't suck anymore. I can't believe you pulled it off."

"I didn't do much," Elle said. "But don't the new uniforms look great? I love the way they pick up the light and splash it all around the gym."

"Maybe the cheerleaders are better," Sidney said. "But the basketball team still reeks." He had planted himself behind Elle, and no matter where she moved, he followed. There wasn't much point in trying to escape him. There were more people in the stands than there had been the week before—mostly guys—but attendance was still pitifully low.

At that moment, Hunter swiped the ball from a Vulture and passed it to one of his teammates, who took an impossible shot and missed. The Vultures snatched up the ball and dribbled it down the court for another basket. The score: 44–10.

A time-out was called. The Killer Bees cheerleaders bounced onto the court to encourage their team.

Ready? Let's go! Time out! Time to shout! We got the spirit, we can't control it! So let it

loose, and rock and roll it! They think they're
tough? Think they can beat us? We'll burn
them, steam them like fajitas! Go, Bees!

While they chanted, the fliers, P.J. and Emma,
were tossed into the air and twirled. They landed
neatly, and the whole squad performed a quick
standing pyramid. When the time-out was over, they
dismounted and ran off the court, to loud applause.
The only problem Elle saw was that Chessie nearly
dropped P.J., who was saved by Savannah at the
last second. But nobody who didn't know the routine would have been likely to notice it.

"That was great," Laurette said. "Too bad the
players have to get back on the court."

Elle's heart sank as she watched the Bees stum
ble all over the court. Hunter made a couple of
beautiful three-point shots and balletic layups, but
the other Bees, when they weren't showboating
and trying in vain to be stars, hardly seemed to
be paying attention. One guy was actually waving
to his girlfriend in the stands as one of Hunter's
passes whizzed by him. There was no teamwork.

"Hey." Laurette poked Elle. "There's Darren."

He was hanging out near the door to the gym,
as if he'd just stopped in to check on the score. But

why would he do that? Nobody cared what the score was. Beverly Hills always lost. When Laurette spotted him, he waved, still very cool, as if it were all just a coincidence.

"He came to see if you were here," Elle said. "Why else would he come?"

"Maybe he likes one of the other girls," Laurette said. "One of the cheerleaders."

"No way," Elle said. "He's not the cheerleader type."

"How do you know?" Laurette asked. "Up until a few weeks ago, you didn't know the first thing about cheerleaders or their types."

"Yeah, but then I watched every cheerleading movie ever made," Elle said. "And in every movie, funky boys like Darren didn't like cheerleaders. Unless the cheerleader was secretly funky, deep down. And trust me, none of these girls are. But in the meantime, here you are, not just secretly funky but openly funky. Look at his T-shirt. You two were made for each other."

Darren's T-shirt said PHIL'S VINTAGE AUTO SHOP and had a picture of an old car from the seventies on it. Elle didn't know what it was called. But she bet Laurette did.

"It's a Ford Torino," Laurette said. "Like the

red-and-white car on *Starsky and Hutch*."

"I knew you'd know," Elle said. "See? I told you that you were made for each other."

"Unfortunately, that's not your decision," Laurette said. "It's his."

"And yours," Elle reminded her.

"I already made up my mind," Laurette said.

"So you haven't talked to him since Amber's party?"

"No. I've seen him around, in the halls and stuff, but he just nods or waves. And I'm too scared to go up and talk to him."

"Why don't you do it now?" Elle asked. "He's just standing there. He looks like he's waiting for you to come over."

"Do you think I should?"

"Yes! Be brave!"

"Okay, I will." Laurette got up and climbed down the bleachers. Darren was watching the game. As Laurette started to walk along the wall toward him, Darren glanced over in Elle's direction, then disappeared out the door.

No! Wait! Elle tried to send him a message through mental telepathy, but that hardly ever worked. *She's coming toward you! You just don't see her! Come back!*

Halfway along the gym wall, Laurette hesitated. Darren was gone. She looked up at Elle. Elle made motions toward the door, trying to tell her to keep going, to go after him. But Laurette was standing right under the basket, and a herd of players was thundering toward her, tumbling out of bounds and fighting over the ball. She retreated and hurried back to Elle.

"You should have gone after him," Elle said.

"It was a stupid idea," Laurette said. "I almost got killed. And being stampeded to death by the Beverly Hills basketball team is not how I want to go."

In spite of the cheerleaders' best efforts, by the end of the game the audience had dwindled to just a few hardy souls. Even most of the players' parents had left. The final score was 75–34. Hunter had scored or assisted on every basket.

"Let's hear it for the Killer Bees!" Savannah shouted; this was met by a chorus of boos and laughter from the visiting fans.

"Now that the cheerleaders are decent, it makes the team seem even more pathetic by comparison," Laurette said.

"Thanks for that helpful observation," Elle said. "Well, time to get to work." She got up to go help

Matt with her assistant-manager duties.

"I'm going home," Laurette said. "Call me later?"

Elle nodded. She waited outside the boys' locker room for the players to finish changing and leave. Mr. Robinson, the basketball coach, paused outside the locker room with a pained look on his face.

"What's wrong, Coach Robinson?" Elle asked.

Coach Robinson shook his head. "I just don't know what to say to these boys anymore," he said. "I think I'll quit coaching after this year."

"Don't do that!" Elle said. "The team has hit rock bottom—there's nowhere to go but up! Things can only get better from here, right?"

"Not if they keep losing," Coach Robinson said, and he went inside the locker room.

Chessie and Chloe were the first cheerleaders to leave the girls' locker room. They sat with Elle and waited for the boys to come out.

"You're still here?" Chessie said. "I would have thought you'd gone home to change for Ryan's party. I mean, nobody would go to a party dressed like that, right?" She looked at Elle's usual baggy pants and sneakers.

"Ryan's having a party?" Elle said.

"Oh, you didn't know?" Chessie said. "Whoops. Sorry. I thought Ryan invited everyone, but I guess not. It just *seems* like he invited everyone."

"That's okay," Elle said. "I have to stay and clean up the locker room anyway."

"Oh, right, because you're assistant manager or something?" Chessie said. "You must be the first girl manager of the boys' team in the history of the school! Go, you! Miss Feminist!"

"Ick, I wouldn't want to touch those dirty towels and stuff," Chloe said.

"Not even Aaron's?" Chessie said. "She has a crush on him," she added, speaking to Elle now. That's why we're hanging here. When he comes out, Chloe's hoping he'll offer her a ride to the party."

"I thought we were here to nab Hunter before Jenna gets to him," Chloe said. "That's what you told me in the locker room."

"What? I told Hunter I'd meet him there. I'm just keeping you company."

"You guys rocked," Elle told them. "You're so good now."

"Thanks," Chloe said.

"Savannah has done wonders with the squad," Chessie said. "It's an honor to be her junior head cheerleader."

The boys started coming out of the locker room, freshly showered. They looked glum. Hunter was the last to leave, and the saddest-looking one of them all.

In spite of what Chessie had said, she didn't leave with Chloe when Aaron offered them a ride. Instead, she stayed and waited for Hunter.

"Those Vultures cheated," Chessie said, running over to him when he appeared. "And did you see their cheerleaders? Arf, arf!"

"You guys are getting so good, though," Hunter said. "Hey, it's you," he added when he noticed Elle. "What happened to your glasses?"

Chessie laughed. "She finally got rid of them! Doesn't she look so much better now? No more Elton John. We'll, maybe a little around the chin—"

"You do look nice," Hunter said to Elle.

"Thanks," Elle said.

"Come on, Hunter, we don't want to keep her." Chessie tugged on his blazer. "She's got work to do! Go on and clean up after everybody, Elle. Scoot!"

Elle watched as Chessie dragged Hunter away. "You guys are going to get better!" she called after them. "I just know you are!"

He glanced back, but Chessie had a firm grip on him and wouldn't let him stop. Matt came out of the locker room. "All clear, Elle," he said. "You can pick up the dirty jerseys and towels while

I go lock the equipment room."

Elle gathered the laundry and left the bag outside for pickup by the laundry service. She thought she could almost smell defeat in the sweaty uniforms—a combination of pessimism and locker-room-boy-stink. It was depressing. She'd brought some air freshener with her—Spring Mist—and sprayed it around the locker room. That made things a little better. She walked past the sinks and the showers, replacing the institutional school soap with a good French lavender soap she'd stolen from the linen closet at home. Lavender was nice and masculine, not too perfumy. She dropped a few scented fabric-softener sheets in with the dirty laundry, too, in hopes that the sweet smell would encourage the players.

That look on Hunter's face—she couldn't get it out of her mind. Desperate, hopeless, and forlorn. Poor Hunter. Poor everyone! This basketball team was dragging the whole school down. The cheerleading squad could be the best in the country, but that wouldn't matter. The team had to win, at least once in a while, to get their self-esteem back and put some pride back in the school.

But how? How would they ever win? Elle didn't know. They'd just have to find a way.

I helped the cheerleaders improve, she thought. Why not the basketball team? I'm no more ignorant about basketball than I was about cheerleading— and I picked that up in a weekend.

That's it, she decided. I'm going to study up on basketball. And, boy, do I have a lot to learn.

But she didn't mind. After all, Hunter loved the sport. And if she were going to be his girlfriend, she'd have to learn to like it, too. It would be a pleasure.

Chapter 11

"SO, A FEW weeks ago you had cheerleader weekend, and now you've got basketball weekend," Laurette said. "What's next, nuclear physics?"

"It's actually pretty cool," Elle said. She had locked herself in her room Saturday morning, just as she had done before, with basketball movies, old game tapes, books, and *Sports Illustrated*. No one but Laurette was allowed to interrupt her, except for the occasional knock from Bernard for food breaks.

"I rented this excellent movie, called *Hoosiers*," Elle said. "Where Gene Hackman comes to this teeny little town in Indiana and turns the pathetic team into state champs? I figure if small-town boys can do it, the sons of movie producers and accountants can do it."

"You're definitely overestimating the sons of movie producers and accountants," Laurette said.

"Look at Michael Jordan." Elle pressed the SLOW MOTION button on her player as he flew through the air, twirling like a ballerina. "Is that not gorgeous?"

"Too bad he's not on our team," Laurette said.

Elle sighed. "I know. It was one thing figuring out how to help the cheerleaders, but improving basketball players—I've got no idea where to start. What we need is a Gene Hackman, a man with a mysterious past, to sweep into town and put some spine in those spoiled boys."

There was a knock on the door, and Bernard came in. "Lunch, girls? Fruit salad, un-turkey sandwiches on rye, and iced tea."

"Thanks, Bernard," Elle said. She and Laurette grabbed the sandwiches and started eating. An old Boston Celtics game played on the TV. Bernard paused. He stood and watched the game.

"No, come on, rebound!" he shouted. "You can't hope to beat Larry Bird if you don't get every rebound."

Elle stopped in midbite and looked up. She'd

never seen Bernard lose his cool, butler-dude composure before.

"Hey, Bernard," she said. "Are you a basketball fan?"

"Certainly, miss," he said. "I once played myself. High school and college."

"I'll bet you were pretty good," Laurette said. Elle noticed with approval that Bernard was extremely tall. She'd noticed that before, of course, but at the time it hadn't mattered much to her. Now she realized she was looking up the nostrils of a real live former basketball player.

"I wasn't bad," Bernard said. "I was recruited for the NBA. But then I hurt my knee and couldn't play seriously anymore. It still creaks when the weather gets humid." He bent and straightened his right knee slightly.

Elle stood up on the bed so she could look right into his eyes. "Wow. So you really know your stuff, right? Bernard, I need your help."

"At your service, miss. What seems to be the problem?"

"Our basketball team is lousy," Laurette said.

"There's one good player—Hunter Perry," Elle said.

"Elle has a crush on him," Laurette said.

"Laurette! TMI! Too much info. Bernard doesn't need to know that."

"Let me guess—Hunter is good, but the rest of the players are not, so Hunter is carrying the whole team on his shoulders?" Bernard said.

"Exactly," Elle said. "Plus, all the other guys take a shot every time they get the ball—and most of the time, they miss. There's no passing, no teamwork, just a bunch of show-offs."

"It just so happens I was in a very similar situation," Bernard said. "I was the tallest player by far on my team, back home in Maine. I grew up in a small town, in more ways than one," Bernard gave a dry laugh. "But we still won most of our games."

"How did you do it?"

"My teammates made sure I had possession of the ball as much as possible," Bernard said. "All our plays were geared toward getting the ball to me at all costs. Then I would simply shoot it, and voilà! Two points. But it required cooperation and intricate teamwork."

"That might work for the Bees," Elle said. "If Hunter had the ball most of the time, he could make more shots. They might even win a game!"

"That's the idea," Bernard said. "The secret is to trick the other team, so they're never sure where the ball is. Fake them out. Otherwise, they all gang up on the star player, and that makes everything more difficult."

"Do you still remember those plays?" Elle asked. "Do you think you could teach them to our team?"

"Some nights I dream about them," Bernard said. "I remember every detail. I would be happy to teach your friends some plays. Though I must warn you, some of them have slightly naughty names. High-school boys' sense of humor, you know."

"Like what?" Elle asked.

"Oh, like the Fred," Bernard said.

"Fred?" Laurette said. "What's so naughty about that?"

"It's an inside joke," Bernard said. "That play was to go up the middle and pick off the ball. We named it after a boy named Fred, who used to pick his nose all the time."

"Eww, Bernard, I never knew you could be gross," Elle said.

"I try not to be," Bernard said. "But you asked."

"Coach Robinson," Elle said after basketball practice Monday, "can I talk to you?"

Elle knew she had to handle the situation

122

delicately. After all, Mr. Robinson was the coach of the team, and she didn't want to suggest that he wasn't doing a good job. It was just that Bernard had specialized experience, and Elle knew he could help. But how would she convince Coach Robinson of that without hurting his feelings?

"Make it sound like you're asking him for a favor," Bibi advised her at Elle's weekly manicure therapy session. "Like you and Bernard are the ones who need *his* help. If he's a decent person, he'll go along with it."

Coach Robinson seemed like a decent person to Elle, so she took Bibi's advice.

"I need your help," she said to him. "I have a friend who used to play basketball, until he hurt his knee. He's been feeling down lately, and I thought it would cheer him up if he could come to one of our practices. Maybe scrimmage with the team a little, show them a couple of his old plays . . . to remind him of his former glory."

Coach Robinson shrugged. "Sure, why not? It's not as if a wasted practice is going to matter much with this team."

Elle thought Coach Robinson was actually the one who needed some cheering up. He must have been so used to losing that he didn't think it was possible to win ever again. "I'm doing you this favor because I appreciate your work as assistant manager, Elle. I don't know why you do it, but it's nice to have you around. Even the locker room smells better since you came along."

Elle was thrilled. "You noticed!"

"The boys noticed, too," Coach Robinson said. "They might not admit it, but I think it boosts their spirits. Even if they can't win a game to save their lives, at least they can smell nice."

"That's my theory, too," Elle said. "Winning isn't everything. Smelling nice counts for a lot."

"You're probably right. So bring your friend along to practice tomorrow afternoon, and we'll see if we can't do a good deed for him."

"Thanks, Coach Robinson. Good deeds pay off sometimes, don't forget."

"Sure they do. Keep dreaming."

"Okay, let's try that again," Bernard shouted. He stood in the middle of the court, surrounded by the five starting players on the basketball team. The bench players watched intently. "The opposing team has their basket well guarded. Hunter, you call the play."

"Bra Stuffer!" Hunter shouted, and the team split

up to cover both sides of the court, while Hunter went for the basket.

"Good," Bernard said. "Now, Wedgie!"

All five players crowded up the middle in a defensive move. Hunter shot and scored.

"Towel Snapper!" Bernard said, as the players snaked the ball along the court until John suddenly snapped it over to Hunter, who took a shot.

"You've got it!" Bernard said. "One more—Panty Raider to Fred!"

"You know, Bernard has a lot more personality than he shows in his butlering work," Laurette said.

"Yeah," Elle said. "I actually thought he was stuffy. This is a real eye-opener for me. I'll never look at him the same way again."

Elle and Laurette sat on the sidelines, watching as Bernard taught the Killer Bees several new plays, all aimed at working as a team to get the ball safely into Hunter's hands. Elle had never seen the team look so energetic. She glanced at Coach Robinson, who was taking notes.

When practice was over, the boys went laughing and joking to the locker room. Elle approached Coach Robinson and said, "Thank you so much. You can't believe what this has done for Bernard. He's like a new man."

"Really? Well, he knows some clever plays." He walked up to Bernard, who was putting on his coat, and shook his hand. "Thank you, sir," Coach Robinson said. "This was the best practice we've had all season. I'll be sure to put your plays into practice."

"You've got some fine players," Bernard said. "All they need is a little motivation."

"Yes, I know," Coach Robinson said. "That's the tough part. When you're dealing with kids who have everything they want . . . Well, they're just not used to working for anything."

"Not every kid in Beverly Hills is spoiled," Bernard said, and he smiled at Elle. "Not beyond repair, anyway."

Chapter 12

"COME ON! Wedgie! Wedgie!" Elle shouted at that Friday's game. The team was doing better at getting the ball to Hunter, but they still seemed lethargic on the court.

"It's so frustrating!" Laurette said. "The plays are good, but there's no energy to back them up."

"At least they're not being totally creamed," Elle said. The score was 43–35, Malibu Martians. Almost respectable.

At halftime the cheerleaders poured onto the court. The Martians went first. They had space-age outfits, complete with antennae, on their heads. They did a lot of flying tricks.

"I like their weirdsmobile shtick," Laurette said.

"Yeah, they're not bad," Elle admitted.

Then the Killer Bees stormed the court. The cheerleaders shouted, *"Bzzz! Bzzz! Have you heard the news? You came all the way from Malibu just to lose! We don't bite, but we sure sting. And we've got the choicest bling! Sting 'em, Bees! Yay!"*

"They're even better than last week," Laurette said. "They're actually about as good as those Martian chicks."

"I know," Elle said. "If Chessie could just keep time a little better; she's always a beat behind."

"She's got a beat behind all right," Laurette said.

"Laurette!" Elle said. "That's not nice. But it is funny."

Laurette smiled and then looked up to see that Darren was making his way through the stands. There were a few more spectators this week than there had been the previous week, due to the word around school about the cheerleaders' sexy new outfits and lack of suckiness. The bleachers were almost a third full. That just about matched the numbers the Malibu team had brought with them. The Bees were making progress.

Darren appeared to be headed right for them. Laurette grabbed Elle's arm. "Oh, my God, Elle, he's coming to sit with us! What do we do?"

"Be cool," Elle said. "This can only be good."

"Cool? Like the way you are every time Hunter is around? You're about as cool as a toaster oven."

"Do as I say, not as I do," Elle said.

Darren sat down right in front of them. "Hey, there," he said, glancing at the scoreboard. "Looks like a good game. The Bees are on the board!"

"What are you doing here?" Laurette asked. "You don't like basketball."

Elle elbowed her. That was not the way to be cool.

"Who says I don't?" Darren said. "I heard Friday night games are the place to be. For the cool kids, anyway."

"Really?" Elle said. "Did you really hear that?"

"Well, I know two cool girls who go every Friday," Darren said. "So I just assumed."

"Oh," Elle said. "You're just flattering us." She cared more about the reputation of the basketball team than about whether or not Darren thought she was cool.

"That's okay—we'll take it," Laurette said. Now it was her turn to elbow Elle.

Elle wanted to kick herself. She and Laurette were so clumsy with boys! They should call themselves Elle and L, the L-bow twins, she thought.

"What are you doing after the game?" Darren asked.

Elle focused her eyes on the court. Hunter was wide open—a perfect opportunity to use the Bra Stuffer play. But Aaron didn't hit his spot in the formation on time, and the Martians overpowered John and wrestled the ball away from him. They dribbled down the court to score.

"Bra Stuffer! Bra Stuffer, you morons!" Elle shouted.

Laurette and Darren stared at her. "What is she talking about?" Darren asked Laurette. "I'd think she'd yell that at the cheerleaders, not the players."

"It's her private language," Laurette said. "Like a code. I don't ask."

"Fourier! Towel Snapper to Hunter! Towel Snapper!" Elle screeched.

"She really gets into it, doesn't she?" Darren said.

"If you only knew," Laurette said. "Anyway, Elle, there's a question on the table. What are we doing tonight?"

"Ribsy is playing the Romper Room," Darren said, when Elle didn't answer. "Some of my buds are going, if you want to tag along." Ribsy was an indie rock band, and the Romper Room was a rock club on Sunset.

"I love Ribsy," Laurette said. "What do you say, Elle?"

Elle wanted to go home and plot some more ways to help the basketball team, but she told herself to snap out of it. The team could wait a day. Darren was asking Laurette on a date, in a roundabout manner. What kind of friend would Elle be if she didn't say yes to help her out?

"I'm there," Elle said.

Darren turned his attention to the court, where the Bees were getting pummeled once again. "Their trouble is they're lazy slobs," Darren said. "That one guy—Kurt—looks like he's afraid to mess up his hair. Except for that Hunter dude. I could watch this team if they were all as good as him."

"I'm so glad you said that," Elle said. "I could talk about that all night."

"But you won't," Laurette said firmly. "Right?"

"Right."

None of the cheerleaders or basketball players went to the Romper Room after the game. They all hung out at a glossier club called Pacifico. The Romper Room was too raw for them. But Elle kind of liked it. It had a children's-playroom-gone-mad vibe, as if a rock star had been let loose in his childhood room and tried to destroy it but not quite managed. The walls were papered with worn old record covers; the bathroom floors were tiled with broken records and CDs; and the furniture was painted with faded pastels of clowns, animals, and flowers, as if for giant children.

Elle sat in an ersatz high chair that was too big for any baby. She watched Darren and Laurette dance on the crowded floor in front of the stage where the band was playing. One of Darren's friends, a scruffy blond guy named Mike, sat next to her, nodding his head to the music.

"Ribsy rocks," he shouted to Elle. "But we rock harder."

"I'd like to see your band sometime," Elle said. Mike was in Warp Factor 5 with Darren. He played drums.

"We haven't had a real gig yet," Mike said. "But you could watch a rehearsal. We practice in my garage."

"Sounds good." Elle thought Mike was okay, if a little spacey, but she actually had no intention of going to his garage to watch a band rehearsal.

"I can't believe Darren went to a basketball game tonight," Mike said. "That is so not like him. He must really dig this chick Laurette."

Elle's ears perked up.

"Yeah," Mike said. "He doesn't talk about stuff like that much, but I know he thinks b-ball is for stiffs. Our team just sucks so bad."

"They're getting better," Elle insisted. She hated to hear people bash the team, but she knew this was the generally accepted opinion around school.

"No way," Mike said. "Those dudes, they all think they're movie stars. Did you ever notice how they walk around school acting as if their lives were one big blockbuster?"

Elle had never thought of it that way, but she could see Mike's point. A lot of the kids at Beverly behaved as if they were constantly being followed by an invisible camera crew.

"Maybe their dad is a movie star's accountant or their mom is dentist to the stars, but that doesn't make them stars themselves," Mike said. "Or even extras. They're living in a fantasy world. It's sad; that's what I think."

"You're right," Elle said, and an idea sprouted in her mind. It was a Beverly Hills quirk—even kids who said they didn't want to act seemed hooked on the idea of stardom. It was most people's reason for being there in the first place—to find stardom, or at least proximity to stardom. It was what motivated everyone in L.A. And motivation was the basketball team's big problem.

But what if the team thought playing well might make them stars?

"Mike, you're brilliant!" Elle kissed him on the cheek before she knew what she was doing. He looked shocked. Elle got up and ran over to Laurette, who was holding hands with Darren. With a feeling that what she was about to say would be a relief to Laurette, Elle said, "I've got to go home. Can you get another ride?"

Laurette glanced at Darren, who nodded. "I was hoping to drive you home anyway."

"Great! Call me later," Elle said. She didn't mind missing the rest of the band. When she got an idea into her head she liked to put it into action as quickly as possible. Otherwise, she felt restless and couldn't sleep. She hurried home to get her idea going before she burst.

Chapter 13

"THE TEAM's improved a lot, Barney." Elle sat at the kitchen table later that night with Bernard and Zosia, having some hot cocoa. Getting the two of them together for the late-night meeting had been the first step in her plan.

She'd grown a lot closer to Bernard since their shared basketball experiences had begun, and felt comfortable calling him Barney now. Even though, with his tall, gray, dignified looks, he really wasn't a Barney. That was what made it fun to call him Barney. And since they were almost buddies, it would make bringing up her plan a lot easier.

"You were right about that boy Hunter," Bernard

said. "He is very talented. He's got a spark the other boys don't have."

"Exactly," Elle said. "And I think I know how to light a fire under their lazy butts. This is where you come in, Zosia," she said, turning to the maid.

"Me? But I don't know anything about basketball."

"That doesn't matter," Elle said. "You can act, I bet. Can't you?"

Zosia preened and fluffed her curly hair. "Well, I think so, but how did you know?"

"I can just tell," Elle said. "The way you move around the house so gracefully. You're not shy, and you're so good at charming repairmen."

"Well, thank you," Zosia said.

"Here's what we do," Elle said. She'd worked it all out in her head on the way home from the Romper Room. "I'll bring you to practice on Monday and say you're a casting agent, a friend of Dad's, and that you're working on a big basketball movie. You're going to hang out at practices and games, because you're scouting for new stars to be in the movie. If the players have a chance to star in a movie, they may actually put some effort into their game. What do you think?"

"Brilliant," Bernard said.

"I like it," Zosia said. "What is the movie called?"

"Um—" Elle hadn't thought about that. "It's tentatively titled—we're only at the preproduction stage, we'll say—*Hoop Nightmares*. No, that's no good. How about, *Fair Net*? Or *Basketball Blues*?"

"I like the last one best," Bernard said.

"We'll say it's about a struggling high-school team whose coach is dying of cancer," Elle said.

"That sounds very real," Zosia said.

"The boys will love you, Zosia," Elle said. "Wear something sexy, and they'll fall all over themselves trying to impress you! If this doesn't motivate them, then they're a lost cause."

"You know something, miss?" Bernard said. "You are becoming very smart."

Elle beamed. "Thank you, Barney."

"Basketball Blues?" Coach Robinson said on Monday afternoon. Elle had gathered the coach and the team together just before practice to introduce them to Zosia. Zosia was dressed in a tight-fitting white suit with a low-cut blouse, high heels, and plenty of makeup. She looked great. Half the team was already drooling just looking at her. Not

Hunter, though. He stood with the ball perched on his hip, scowling.

"That's right," Elle said. "And this is Lisa LaRue. She's a friend of my father's. She's the casting director in charge of *Basketball Blues*, and she's looking for unknown talent. She needs at least twenty high-school players for the movie, and when Dad told her about the Beverly Hills team, she just had to come and see you. Lisa?"

"Thank you, Elle, darling," Zosia said. "Isn't she a sweetheart? Now, boys, I'm not looking for good looks, particularly. I'm looking for boys who can play. And teamwork. If I can cast a whole team, it will save us that much more time during shooting, because we won't have to train you to play together. And as you know, time is money. Or maybe you don't know it, but I'm telling you now. Time is money."

"Lisa will come to practices and games to watch you," Elle said.

"Don't you think this might be a little distracting?" Hunter said. "I don't care about being in a movie. I just want to play."

Elle's heart fluttered. Hunter was pure. He wasn't driven by a lust for fame and attention. He just wanted to play. It made her love him more.

"Lisa will sit quietly in the stands," Elle explained. "She won't say much. Just try to ignore her. Forget she is there. Okay?"

The boys stared blankly at Zosia. It was clear that, except for Hunter, they would never be able to forget she was there. That was just what Elle was hoping.

"So, go on! Play! Practice!" Zosia said. "And thank you for your help."

"Our pleasure, Miss LaRue," Coach Robinson said. "You don't happen to be casting the role of the coach, by the way, do you?"

"We're in discussion with Tom Hanks," Zosia said. "But we haven't agreed to anything yet, so you never know."

"Tom Hanks!" a few of the boys murmured.

"Yes," Zosia said. "And Scarlett Johansson will play the girlfriend of one of the players. Oh, and Paris Hilton will play a cheerleader."

"Paris Hilton playing a cheerleader?" one of the boys muttered. "Awesome!"

Coach Robinson clapped his hands. "Come on, boys, let's get moving!"

Elle and Zosia sat in the stands to watch the practice. The boys warmed up by running up and down the bleachers until they could hardly breathe.

Elle had never seen them do that before. They did push-ups and crunches, then drills and scrimmages. The boys sank basket after basket. After each swish, they glanced toward Zosia to see if she were watching.

"I think it's working," Elle said to Zosia as they watched from the stands. "I've never seen them work out so hard. If they work this hard all week, maybe they'll actually win the game this Friday." Elle checked the schedule. "They're playing the Hollywood Hulks. The name is deceiving—they're not that big. They're just really into comic books. They're actually one of the weaker teams in the C-Conference. We might have a chance."

"So I get to come here every day and sit and watch these boys play?" Zosia said.

"You don't mind, do you?"

"Not at all," Zosia said. "It beats watching *Divorce Court* with your mother while I fold the laundry and she gets riled up over what jerks all the husbands are. You did clear this with Eva, didn't you? She hates to watch *Divorce Court* alone."

"Not exactly, but I'm sure she'll go along with it," Elle said. "If I tell her you're helping me get a Prom date, she won't care if we're robbing liquor stores."

"You're right," Zosia said. "And anyway, she owes me one."

"For what?"

"For getting rid of your glasses," Zosia said. "I made one of her dreams come true. So she can manage a few episodes of *Divorce Court* without me."

Chapter 14

TWEEEEEET! "Time-out!"

The ref blew his whistle, and the cheerleaders bounded on to the court. It was the final period of the game: Killer Bees versus the Hulks, and the score was tied at 55–55 with fifty seconds left to go. Elle gripped Zosia's hand in her right and Laurette's in her left.

"This is blowing my mind," Laurette said. "The Bees could actually win this game."

"Shhh! Quiet!" Elle said. "You might jinx them!"

"They're really not so bad, Elle," Zosia said. "I thought you said they were bad."

"Time-out!" the cheerleaders chanted. *"It's time to shout! We got that spirit, we can't control it, so let*

it loose and rock and roll it! We're the best, we can't be beat. We'll rock this joint to your defeat! GO, KILLER BEES!"

"They sound like they actually mean it this time," Laurette said.

The bleachers were less than half full, but that was a big improvement over the week before. And the people in the crowd were on the edge of their seats.

The players returned to the floor. The Killer Bees flawlessly executed one of Bernard's plays—the Second Baser—and passed the ball to Hunter. He shot from half-court as the seconds ticked away. Five, four, three . . .

Swish! The ball went in. The buzzer sounded. Game over. The Killer Bees had won!

Elle jumped up and down, screaming and hugging Zosia and Laurette. "We won! We won! We won a game! We did it!"

The Beverly Hills bleachers went crazy. The Hollywood Hulk fans sat in stunned silence on their side. They had surely thought this game was a given. And considering Beverly's 0–6 record, it would be hard to blame them. But they were wrong. Gloriously, brilliantly wrong.

The Beverly Hills crowd ran on to the court to

celebrate with the players, who were out of their minds with joy. Elle watched Hunter's face glow with happiness as he hugged his teammates. She wished he would hug her, too. She wished she had the guts to go over to him and throw her arms around him, throw caution to the wind, who cared what he thought? But she didn't go. Not this time.

"Hey, everybody," John Fourier yelled. "Party at my house! Let's celebrate!"

Elle was wearing her blue-and-gold assistant manager T-shirt over her usual baggy pants. "I guess you can wear that thing proudly now, instead of hiding it under a sweatshirt or something," Laurette said, nodding her head at Elle's T.

"I was always proud of this shirt," Elle insisted. "But it is nicer to wear it after a win. Our first win of the season!" She hugged Laurette again. She was so excited she couldn't stop hugging people.

"Elle, if you don't stop hugging me we'll both get calluses on our arms," Laurette joked.

They were standing near the bar at John Fourier's pool house, clutching big plastic cups of soda. Zosia had gone home. She'd felt funny about going to a high-school party, and she had also been afraid the boys would swamp her with questions about

Basketball Blues, for which she had no answers. She didn't mind lying a little bit, but she tried to keep it to a minimum.

The pool house and the trees around it were covered with tiny lights, and tiki torches illuminated the pool itself. The basketball players and cheerleaders and other Beverly Hills students were so excited about the win they couldn't stop whooping, yelling, and jumping around. Savannah was talking to Bryce, her lacrosse player, who, as always, was twirling a ball in a lacrosse stick. Elle kept her eye on Hunter, who stood inside a circle of teammates, surrounded by a second circle of admiring cheerleaders recounting every minute of the game.

"Don't you know what this means?" Elle whispered to Laurette. "My plan is working! No one thought the Bees would win a game, and now they have! And they can win more games, too! And if that can happen—something that everybody (even you, admit it) thought was totally impossible, then anything can happen. Even Hunter asking me to the Prom."

"But you understand that those are two totally separate things," Laurette said. "The basketball team winning and you going to the Prom. Not related."

"They're not *un*related," Elle insisted.

"I'm not going to argue about it," Laurette said. "Let me just go on record as saying that I disagree."

"Everyone's entitled to her opinion," Elle said.

"Maybe you could give me your opinion on *my* chances," Laurette said.

"Your chances with what?"

"It's a secret, but I have a Prom dream of my own," Laurette said.

Elle grinned. "Darren?"

Laurette nodded. "I really like him, Elle. He's a senior. He can go to Prom. If only he'd ask me—"

"He will!" Elle squealed. "I know he will. It will be so perfect. We'll both go to Prom with the boys we love! It will be the best night of our lives!"

"We'll see," Laurette said. "I think he kind of likes me. We danced a lot at that club last weekend."

"He's totally into you," Elle assured Laurette. She was so happy. If her best friend could go to Prom with her, it would make it a billion times more fun.

"But it's not like we're boyfriend or girlfriend or anything," Laurette said. "It's not a given."

"Who else would he ask? You're perfect for him. You look like you belong together, two groovy, vintage-wearing hipsters."

Laurette suddenly froze. "Don't look now, but here he comes."

"Who? Darren?"

"No, silly."

Elle looked and saw Hunter ambling toward them. He looked even more handsome than usual, his black hair still damp from his postgame shower, his blue button-down shirt half tucked into his jeans in just the right way.

"Hunter! Congratulations!" Elle said. "You guys were awesome tonight. It was just like *Hoosiers*."

"Thanks." Hunter smiled modestly yet proudly. Not an easy trick to pull off. "You've seen *Hoosiers*?"

"Of course," Elle said. "It's my new favorite movie. You remind me of that kid Jimmy, the best player in the history of Indiana basketball."

"Wow, thanks," Hunter said. "That's my favorite movie, too."

His eyes glittered in the torchlight. He glanced at Elle's T-shirt. "So, Assistant Manager, I guess you ditched your glasses for good, huh?"

"Yeah. I've got contacts now," Elle said. "What do you think?"

"You have pretty eyes," Hunter said. "Glasses-free is definitely the way to go."

Elle caught her breath. He had said she had

pretty eyes! She could die now. But Laurette wouldn't let her. And Laurette was right. She had too much to live for.

"Did you guys learn some new plays, or what?" Laurette asked, baiting the hook.

"Actually, we did," Hunter said. "And they helped a lot. This tall dude named Bernard came to practice one day—wasn't he, like, a friend of yours or something?"

"He's a family friend," Elle said.

"Cool guy," Hunter said. "Really knows his stuff."

"I loved the way you did that Latrell Spread-Eagle Sinker," Elle said. "And that Wes Unseld charge down the court—beauty!"

Hunter looked at her in surprise. "You know about Wes Unseld? He played on the Bullets almost forty years ago."

"Sure," Elle said. "I love basketball. Those old games are more exciting than the new ones, in a way. And some of those seventies uniforms are way cooler than the baggy shorts they wear now. How do you know about Wes?"

"I studied his old games," Hunter said. "I figured I might catch some moves there that the other teams won't have seen before. But Barney knew some even more obscure plays. And they worked."

He started looking at her in a funny way. As if he were seeing her for the first time.

"I'm going to go get another drink," Laurette said. "Anybody want anything?"

Elle absently shook her head. She was caught in the tractor beam of Hunter's gaze.

"You know, ever since you became our assistant manager," Hunter began, "things have begun to change. The cheerleaders got way better. And then this mysterious tall dude teaches us some great new plays. Then there's your other family friend, the casting agent . . . Ever since she started coming to practice, the other guys have gotten off their butts and put in a little effort."

Elle felt a shiver of excitement. He noticed!

"And then we win our first game," Hunter said. "You're really involved with the team. What are you, some kind of fairy godmother?"

"Godmother? No, I'm too young for that," Elle said.

"What's your name again?" Hunter asked.

"Elle. Elle Woods."

"Good to know you, Elle Woods," Hunter said.

"It's really good to know you, Hunter Perry." Elle knew that sounded gushy, but she couldn't stop herself. She was having a real conversation with Hunter! He was paying attention to her, and now he knew her name!

"Elle!" Chessie's high-pitched voice pierced through the sweetness of the moment. She came over, dressed in a short yellow cotton sundress very similar to one that Savannah had worn a few days earlier. She put her arm around Elle. "Isn't she adorable?" Chessie said to Hunter. She plucked at Elle's T-shirt. "Assistant manager. Imagine, a girl managing a boys' team. Well, *assisting* the manager. That's dedication. I admire a girl who doesn't mind doing everyone else's dirty work. I say that to our cleaning lady almost every day: how much I admire her for all the icky, filthy, yucky stuff she's willing to do, just for us."

"It's not that bad," Elle said.

"Well, all I know is, I couldn't bear to smell like a bunch of sweaty athletic socks." She leaned close to Elle, sniffed her neck, and wrinkled her nose. "It's hard to get that smell out, isn't it? That's the trouble. No matter how many showers you take, you just can't get that sweaty sock smell off your skin. You should come to the girls' locker room next time, Elle. I've got this shampoo that smells so good, maybe it could get rid of that smell."

Elle took a deep breath in. "I don't smell anything," she said.

"Well, you wouldn't, because you're used to it," Chessie said.

"I don't smell anything, either," Hunter said.

"You're sweet to say that," Chessie said. She took Hunter by the arm and started to lead him away. "Savannah wants to ask you something. Did you have a chance to watch any of our cheers tonight? We were wondering if you thought the last pyramid was working. . . ."

"I really don't have time to watch cheers during the game," Hunter said as Chessie dragged him away. Elle stared forlornly after them. Laurette reappeared with her fresh drink.

"Chessie officially has the worst timing," Elle said, taking a sip of her drink.

"Elle, if you want Hunter to ask you to the Prom, you've got more work to do," Laurette said. "There are lots of obstacles in your way. And Chessie is one of the biggest."

"Because Hunter likes her?" Elle asked.

"I don't know whether he likes her or not," Laurette said. "But she likes him, and she's ruthless. She'll do whatever she has to to snag that Prom date. And I get the feeling she'll stoop about as low as anyone can go. Are you willing to out-stoop her?"

"Don't be silly, Laurette," Elle said. "That won't be necessary. True love always wins in the end—don't you know that?"

"No, I don't know that," Laurette said. "Chessie's pulling a Savannah—purposely putting you down in front of other people to raise herself up."

"What? But Savannah's so nice," Elle said.

"She's nice to *you*," Laurette said. "She likes you, because you've helped her. But have you ever noticed how she's always dissing Chessie? And she's not super friendly to me, either."

"Well, I know Chessie still looks up to Savannah, even though she isn't super nice to her," Elle said. She watched as Savannah and Chessie laughed at something Hunter said. He looked very happy in their company. "She wants to be like her. And maybe that's not so dumb. After all, Hunter went out with Savannah for two years. Maybe she's his type."

"And Chessie thinks that being like Savannah will make Hunter like her more," Laurette said.

"Savannah is beautiful and popular," Elle said. "And confident. She acts like a queen. Like she expects people to do what she wants."

"And they do," Laurette said.

"Maybe Chessie is on to something," Elle said. "Maybe Hunter *does* like that type."

"It sure looks that way," Laurette said. Chessie had her hand on Hunter's arm, and he didn't seem to mind one bit.

"It wouldn't kill me to be a little more like Savannah," Elle said. "If I can figure out the secret of her appeal, it might make Hunter fall for me."

"That's a tall order," Laurette said. "I mean, who wouldn't want to be like Savannah? And yet there's only one."

"Well, get ready, because from now on there are going to be two," Elle said. She took a sip of soda and accidentally snorted it up through her nose. She coughed and managed to choke it down. Laurette patted her on the back.

"Good luck, Elle. You're going to need it."

Chapter 15

"WHAT IS she like, this girl Savannah?" Bibi asked. Elle was relaxing at her weekly appointment. Thank goodness for manicures! How had she ever lived without them?

"She's beautiful," Elle said. "She's tall, with long blonde hair, and slim and athletic. And she has green eyes and this tiny, perfect nose . . . and she's really nice. To me, anyway. She's the head cheer-leader, but she was the only one who would listen to me at first about fixing up the squad. She thinks I'm cute. That's what she says, anyway. Everybody wants to be like her. And everybody wants her to like them. It's like she has this *power*—"

"Hmmm." Bibi was giving Elle a sophisticated

French manicure this week. "And she dated Hunter for two years? Why did they break up?"

"I don't know," Elle said. "It's kind of a mystery. Neither one of them really talks about it."

"Let me ask you this," Bibi said. "Does Savannah boss people around a lot? Does she automatically expect everyone to do what she wants?"

"Well, yes, I guess so."

"Does she walk around as if she's wearing an invisible tiara on her head?"

"Yes! I never thought about it that way before," Elle said. "But she does. And it looks good on her, too."

"I know the type," Bibi said. "She sounds just like Mary Jo Bennett, my head cheerleader when I was in high school. They're all alike. I used to be so intimidated by her! I wanted to be just like her. I tried cutting my hair like hers, and talking like her, and imitating everything she did. But nothing worked. Then, during senior year, I finally figured out her secret."

Elle was spellbound. "What was it?"

"She never showed weakness," Bibi said. "She never let anyone get to her. Or if they did, no one ever found out. She was an ice princess. Well, I'm sorry, but I just can't pull that off. I can try to be cool or whatever, but if I'm mad, you're going to hear about it; and if I'm happy, I'll jump for joy; and if something bugs me, it shows right on my face. That's just the way I was born, and I can't do anything to change it."

"Wow," Elle said. "You're right. Savannah is always in control. Nothing ever seems to surprise her. I wonder if I could be that way, if I practiced?"

"If you really want to be like Savannah, there's one other secret you should know," Bibi said. "Clothes. Every ice princess needs a wardrobe to back her up. Her authority comes from her invulnerability and from always wearing the exact perfect thing. They use fashion like a suit of armor."

"Clothes, huh?" Elle looked down at her grubby T-shirt, her paint-spattered sweatpants, her worn-out old sneakers. She had to admit that now that she was always perfectly manicured, even she had noticed that her clothes didn't quite work. Still, she had resisted changing her style.

"But these clothes are so comfortable," she said, though she knew it was a lost cause. They had to go.

"Nice clothes can be comfortable, too, once you get used to them," Bibi said. "You would look so adorable in, say, a robin's-egg-blue cotton button-down with white capri pants and matching blue mules! So adorable!"

"My mother has been bugging me for ages to let her take me shopping," Elle said.

"There you go!" Bibi said. "Take her up on it! You'll bond. She'll love it. And it's fun, you'll see. Oh, I can't wait to see what you'll be wearing when you come in for your appointment next week!"

"Don't get your hopes up, Bibi," Elle said. "I'll still be the same old Elle."

"Of course you will," Bibi said. "Only better."

"Better," Elle said. The same old Elle with a little bit of Savannah thrown in. How could it hurt? Everyone could use a touch of Savannah, right? It was what Elle wanted, after all—to be the kind of girl Hunter liked. Like Savannah.

Eva squeezed Elle for the fortieth time that afternoon. "I'm so excited, honey! You've finally come to your senses."

"Calm down, Mom," Elle said. She was glad she could make her mother happy, but she wished Eva would stop squeezing the air out of her.

"You, too, Laurette," Eva said. It was Tuesday after school, and Eva had taken Elle and Laurette to some of the swankiest shops in Beverly Hills. "It's a girl date! Don't you love it?"

Laurette rolled her eyes at Elle, who giggled. Eva meant well. And it was nice of her to buy all those clothes for the girls. Already Elle had gotten three new school outfits, two party dresses, a designer bag, and a pair of very cool sunglasses. Laurette had found designer versions of the vintage clothes she loved. They were like her usual clothes, only better, with hipper colors and a better fit.

Elle was beginning to get the hang of this shopping thing. Actually, she took to it like a pro. She could see why everybody raved about it so much. It was like a game.

"Mom! Those Gucci sandals!" She pointed to a pair of gold flats in the shoe department of the high-end store they were currently browsing through.

"Love them!" Eva cried. "They scream, 'evening pool party'!"

"We never go to evening pool parties," Laurette pointed out.

"You will if you have those sandals," Eva said.

"It could happen," Elle said. "Weren't we just at John Fourier's last weekend? And what about Amber's Malibu beach party?"

"That was a fluke," Laurette said.

"It wasn't a fluke," Elle said. "It was the beginning of a new era for us. Elle and L, the Party Years." Laden with shopping bags, they wandered through the maze of cosmetics counters on the first floor. A young man stopped them and sprayed perfume on their wrists. "Free sample," he said.

"Try our new High Shine Lip Lacquer?" a young woman asked. She beckoned from behind a glossy counter. Another saleswoman hovered over a customer sitting on a high stool as she put makeup on her.

"Girls," Eva said, "this is a sign from above. Makeover!" She dragged Elle and Laurette to the counter.

"Mom, I don't know," Elle protested. "Let's not go crazy—"

"No more resisting," Eva said. "Park it! And I'll have one, too, while we're here. One's face can always use freshening up."

She and the girls perched on stools at the counter as salesgirls cooed over them. "We'll try this very light foundation on you," Elle's makeover artist, a pretty Asian woman, said. "You have lovely skin, so you don't need much." She stepped back, looked Elle over, and started brushing something on her face. "For you, I'd play up the eyes. All the way. That and a little lip gloss is all you need, but you'll see—it will make a big difference."

"It will polish up her look, right?" Eva said.

"Exactly," the woman said.

Fifteen minutes later, Elle's face was finished. Elle looked at Laurette. Laurette's dark eyebrows had been tweezed and shaped; blusher brought out her sharp cheekbones, and her full lips were covered in a cherry-red lipstick that went perfectly with her vintage look—very forties.

"Laurette, you look fabulous!" Elle said.

"So do you!" Laurette said. They stared at the mirror together. Elle didn't appear to be wearing much makeup, but she had to admit she looked prettier than usual. Her blue eyes seemed enormous, and her skin glowed.

"You both look beautiful," Eva said. She was wearing a new coral shade of lipstick that brought out her tan. "You should listen to me more often, Elle. Admit that I was right all along—come on, admit it," she said playfully.

"I admit it," Elle said. "Mother knows best."

"It only took you sixteen years to figure it out," Eva said. She smiled and bought the makeup Elle and Laurette needed to create their looks at home.

"Wait until Hunter sees you now," Laurette said. "He'll fall all over himself to ask you to the Prom."

"And Darren will ask you, too," Elle said. "And everything will be perfect! Just like a fairy tale."

"Wow, girls," Eva said. "Makeup is a powerful tool, but I don't know if it's *that* strong."

"It has to be," Elle said. "If all this doesn't work, what else is left to try?"

Chapter 16

"ELLE, ARE you aware that you've been looking kind of different lately?" Sidney said to her in homeroom the next morning. She was wearing her new capri pants with an off-the-shoulder pink top, her makeup was artfully applied (Zosia had helped her) and her hair neatly pulled back. She felt great. She had noticed the stares in the hallway as she walked into school with Laurette that morning. Shocked, bemused stares from the girls and appreciative, hot-mama stares from the boys. She had to admit, that Bibi knew her stuff.

"Different how?" she asked.

"Well, I always thought you were the most scrumptious girl I ever saw," Sidney said. "And now, somehow, you look more yummy than ever. Is it a magic potion? What is it?"

Elle was getting a case of the icks at Sidney's talking about her as if she were food. But what would Savannah do? She'd be an ice princess. Keep her cool. So Elle kept her cool.

"It's just some new clothes, no big deal," Elle said.

"You look like strawberry ice cream," Sidney said.

"Okay, that's enough," Elle said. Going into ice-princess mode was easy around Sidney. If only she could pull it off with Hunter.

"Elle, are you on a new diet or something?" Chloe asked later that day. The cheerleaders were practicing a new routine, and Elle was watching for a few minutes before going back to basketball practice to help Matt chase stray balls. "You look way hot."

"Yeah, I love your shoes," Jenna said. "Miu-Miu?"

"Marc Jacobs," Elle said.

"Even Laurette looked somewhat human today," Chloe said. "What's with you two?"

"Looks to me like somebody finally got her first credit card," Chessie said. "Poor Elle—didn't anyone tell you? The off-the-shoulder look is so over. But of course they *wouldn't* tell you at the store—they're trying to unload all their unwanted stuff on unsuspecting chumps."

Elle plucked self-consciously at her top. She'd loved the way it looked in the store—was it really so out of date? She didn't think so. She'd seen several models wearing them in the magazines she read.

"These things are cyclical," Savannah said. "I heard off-the-shoulder is coming back strong. So Elle's look is actually fashion-forward."

Elle smiled gratefully at Savannah. How did she always know the right thing to say? How did she always seem to know everything?

"You look great, Elle," Savannah said. "Spending time around me must be rubbing off on you. You're like my little apprentice. My mini-me."

Chessie scowled. Elle felt sorry for her. She knew Chessie wanted to be Savannah's mini-me. Who wouldn't? But for some reason Savannah just wouldn't cut her a break. It had to hurt. Elle decided to try to make Chessie feel better.

"You always look nice, too, Chessie," Elle said. "Lots of times I've noticed you wearing the same thing as Savannah, and you almost pull it off!"

"Wooo!" the other girls said, as if Elle had said something catty. Had she? She hadn't meant to! She had really been trying to be nice. After all, no one could expect to wear the same thing as Savannah and look just as good as Savannah did. It was impossible.

Chessie was speechless. She looked as if she were going to explode.

"Get a grip, Chessie, she's only saying to your face what everybody's been saying behind your back all year," Savannah said. "You're a copycat. You've got no style of your own."

"Savannah! How can you say that? I've got the same style as you!"

"Whatever." Savannah clapped her hands. "Come on, everybody, let's practice. We actually won a game last week! Let's get psyched!"

"Look at you, gorgeous!" Bibi exclaimed. Elle had stopped by Pamperella to show Bibi her new look. "So sophisticated! A real Beverly Hills babe."

"Thanks," Elle said.

"It really suits you," Bibi said. "You know? It's clear you've always had an eye for color and design, and now the whole world can see it. I'm glad you dropped by to surprise me, because *I* have a surprise for *you*. I'll be right back."

Bibi retreated to the employee lounge and returned carrying a tiny bundle in her arm. She held it out to Elle. "To complete your new look. And a new friend for you."

Elle took the little bundle. It was a tiny Chihuahua. Elle gasped. "Kitty had her puppies! Oh, Bibi, he's adorable!"

"I thought you'd like him."

Kitty trotted past, rubbing against Elle's leg. Elle reached down to pet her.

"Thank you, Kitty. And thank you, Bibi. I promise to take good care of him."

"What will you name him?" Bibi asked.

Elle stared into the dog's tiny, mouselike face. He licked her finger. She fell completely in love. "He's so fragile, but I'll make sure he grows up strong," Elle said. "Even if he is a late bloomer, like me. I think I'll name him Underdog."

"You two were made for each other," Bibi said.

"You know what we need, Underdog?" Elle said, looking at the puppy's face. "We need a good tote bag to carry you around in. I'm going to take you everywhere."

She drove to Chanel and bought the perfect tote-dog carrier, all furry and padded inside, but with tiny airholes for breathability. She put Underdog in it and he rode along with her in the bag as she walked happily down the sunny street. Just ahead, she spotted Laurette and Darren sitting at a sidewalk café, having coffee. She was so excited about her new puppy she didn't think about what that meant: *Darren and Laurette having coffee together.*

"Laurette!" Elle cried. "Look what Bibi gave me." She presented Underdog to Laurette and Darren.

"He's so cute!" Laurette gently stroked the puppy's head.

"Hey, little dude," Darren said.

"I'm going to make a sweet little sweater for him tonight," Elle said. "He'll be the best-dressed dog in town."

She ordered a coffee before it dawned on her: was she interrupting something? She glanced at Laurette, who looked perfectly happy and not annoyed at all.

Darren's cell phone rang. "It's Mike. I'd better take it." He got up from the table and walked a little bit away from the girls for privacy. They could just hear him say, "Mike, dude, did you hear anything yet?"

"They sent a demo CD to the Romper Room," Laurette explained. "To see if they can get a gig there. Mike was supposed to hear from them today." She leaned forward and grabbed Elle's hand. "Elle! He asked me out!"

"On a date?" Elle gasped. This was giant news!

"Yes, on a date," Laurette said. "To the movies. This Saturday!"

"That's fantastic!" Elle squealed. "I told you he likes you! We're going to be Prom buddies; you wait and see."

Darren came back and sat down. "We didn't get the gig. They said they're booked for the next couple of months, but maybe after that . . ." He looked disappointed. "We're so ready to play. But it's hard to get a gig if you've never played anywhere else."

"You'll get one somewhere soon," Laurette said.

"There are so many bands in L.A.," Darren said. "The competition is brutal." He sighed. "I was really looking forward to playing in front of a real audience for the first time."

"There are lots of other things to look forward to," Elle said. "Like the basketball championships. Will the Killer Bees take it all the way?"

Both Darren and Laurette looked at Elle as if she were crazy. "The championship? Come on," Darren said. "They'll never make it."

"You have to admit it's a long shot," Laurette said.

"Stranger things have happened," Elle said. "I think they can do it."

"I wouldn't bet on it," Darren said. "Unless you like to lose."

"Okay, so you don't share my visions of glory. One step at a time. What about the game Friday night?" Elle said. "The suspense is killing everyone—can the Bees do it again?"

Darren made a face. Unfortunately, skepticism was still the prevailing attitude of most Beverly Hills students. So the team had won once—it had to be a fluke, right?

"Well, and there's Prom," Elle said. "You're a senior. Aren't you looking forward to one of the most romantic nights of your high-school life?"

Laurette, beaming, propped her elbows on the table and waited for his answer. Maybe he'd ask her then and there! Elle hoped so. Then the friends could both relax and focus on the bigger challenge: Hunter.

But Darren said, "The Prom? You must be kidding."

Elle sat up. "Why would I be kidding? I don't kid about things like the Senior Prom."

"I'm not going to any stupid dance," Darren said. "I'm philosophically against proms."

Laurette's face fell. She was upset, Elle could tell, but she tried to hide it. She opened her backpack and pretended she was looking for something until she recovered her composure. That was Laurette's nothing-hurts-me trick.

"How can you be philosophically against proms?" Elle asked. "What have they ever done to you?"

Darren shrugged. "Nothing. I just think they're meant for the other kids at school, the jocks and the cheerleaders and all those types. They're not very rock."

"They can be rock," Elle said. "It depends what the theme is."

"Whatever," Darren said. "I'll make sure I have other plans that night. Maybe Laurette and I can rent a movie or something."

Laurette smiled wanly. "Yeah. Sure. That would be fun."

"Rent a movie?" Elle was outraged. "You can do that any old night. Your Prom only comes once in a lifetime."

"It's no big deal," Darren said. "Right, Laurette?"

"Right," Laurette said, but Elle could see the disappointment on Laurette's face.

"Laurette," Elle said. "You know you want to go."

"I do not," Laurette said. "Like Darren said, it's no big deal."

Laurette was lying, Elle knew. She didn't want

to seem uncool in front of Darren, not when they hadn't even had their first date yet.

If Beverly Hills High had a school-spirit deficit, Darren was one of the leading reasons for it. But that could change.

Elle would find a way.

Chapter 17

KURT PASSED to Hunter, who, as if in slow motion, leaped into the air and dunked the ball. Elle sighed happily. Hunter playing ball was a thing of beauty.

"Final score, fifty-four to fifty. The Bees win again!"

Elle, Laurette, and Zosia jumped up and down and cheered at Friday night's exciting game. The cheerleaders were totally on, and the players were hotter than ever. Elle was so excited she even hugged Sidney, who was sitting, uninvited, on her other side.

"They won again!" Zosia cried.

"They've totally turned the season around," Laurette said.

"They could make it to the championships if they keep this up," Elle said. "For real! I knew they could do it!"

"They haven't done it yet," Sidney reminded her. "And the bleachers still aren't full."

"Sidney, why did you come here if all you're going to do is tear the team down?" Elle asked.

"To be with you," he said. "And because I hope that by tearing the team down you will start to like me instead."

"That will never work," Elle told him. She studied the crowd as people filed happily out of the gym. "But you have a point, Sidney. There's a whole group at school—a big group—that never come to games, because they don't like sports."

"You mean the geeks?" Laurette said.

"Exactly," Elle said. "If they came to the games, the stands would be packed, and the gym would be rocking every game night. Team morale would skyrocket. They couldn't lose!"

"You'll never get the geeks to come," Sidney said. "They hate sports."

"Maybe something else could draw them," Elle said. "Something we're missing. I've noticed that the other teams have marching bands. Where's ours?"

"I guess there isn't enough interest," Sidney said.

"You're in the school band, aren't you, Sidney?" Elle said.

"Yeah, but we're very serious. We don't do half-time shows."

"Why not? Halftime shows can be great," Elle said. "All you have to do is use your imagination."

"If a good geeky band was playing, the nerds would come to the games," Laurette said. "I mean, I guess they would. I'm trying to put myself in the mind of a nerd. It's not too much of a stretch for me, frankly."

"I just don't think they'll be interested," Sidney said. "Why would we want to support a bunch of jocks who get too much attention already? It's not the geek way."

"Do you have band practice on Monday?" Elle asked.

Sidney nodded.

"Let me talk to them," she said. "I bet I can get them to do it. And with a great team, a great cheerleading squad, and a decent marching band, we'll be unbeatable! The whole school will be involved. It will transform Beverly Hills High."

"That's a pretty ambitious plan for a tasty little morsel like you," Sidney said.

Elle looked to Laurette to play the heavy for her.

"Zip it, Sidney," Laurette said.

"A marching band?"

When Elle first presented the idea to the school band, it didn't go over well. The band was made up of thirty serious musicians who aspired to play in a concert hall, not a gym.

"Sure," Elle said. "It will be fun. It's not as if you've got a huge following otherwise. Think of it as free advertising."

"We don't know any marching-band music," a greasy-haired trombone player said. His name was Merlin, and he was the leader of the band.

"We did play 'The Stars and Stripes Forever' once," a girl drummer said. "But we mostly play classical favorites like *Peter and the Wolf* or the *1812* Overture."

"Those are nice," Elle said uncertainly. She had a vague idea that those tunes were not very funky. "What other songs do you know?"

"Stravinsky's *Firebird*."

"Pachelbel's Canon in D."

"'The Waltz of the Flowers.'"

"Uh-huh," Elle said. "Um, don't you know any *good* songs?"

"Like what?" the drummer asked.

"Like, 'Jungle Boogie,'" Elle suggested. "Or 'Get the Party Started.' Something like that?"

Silence.

"'Flight of the Bumblebee'?" Elle tried. At least that had a connection with the team's name.

"We know that one," the clarinetist said. "But why would we want to play dance music?"

"I'll tell you why," Elle said. "To get the crowd moving. To whip up their spirits. To help the team win."

"If the team can't win without us, they're in trouble," someone said.

"Listen," Elle said. "You've got the wrong attitude. Think about what I'm offering you here. You will be playing during the breaks with the cheerleaders. Haven't the boys among you secretly dreamed of dating a cheerleader? Now's your chance! You can be part of the big championship basketball team. The focus of the entire school. The stars! The heroes! I can't understand why anyone wouldn't want to be a part of that."

The oboist snorted. "Championship team? What are you talking about? We've never won a basketball championship before, and we never will."

"You're wrong," Elle said. "But, okay, don't

believe me. Even if the team doesn't make it, you'll still be about a hundred times cooler than you are now. Admit it—your social stock has nowhere to go but up."

The band members glanced at one another. They tried to pretend they didn't care about things like being cool, but they were high-school students like everybody else, and susceptible to temptation.

"Cheerleaders . . ." Elle said once again, dangling a picture of the squad in front of them.

The band members huddled together, whispering. Finally, Merlin said, "All right, Elle. You've got a marching band."

Chapter 18

"GOOD LUCK at the game tonight, Hunter," Elle said. She'd "bumped into him"—another way of saying, "staked him out"—outside the gym on Friday night as he went inside to change for the game. "Give me an *H*! Give me a *U*!—"

"Uh, thanks." Hunter glanced at her uncertainly. She was wearing her Killer Bees jacket over low-rise jeans and a cool embroidered top. "You're Elle, right? The assistant manager? You look different."

"I do? That's funny. Anyway, I want you to meet someone." Elle opened her doggy tote bag to reveal Underdog's tiny ears. "Come on out and say hello, Underdog."

The puppy poked his head out. "Look—I made

him a little yellow-and-black-striped sweater and these cute little fuzzy antennae." She pulled Underdog out of the bag to show off his costume. "He's a Killer Bee!"

Hunter laughed. He reached for Underdog's little paw and shook it.

"Nice to meet you, Underdog."

"Wait until you see the big surprise I've got for everybody tonight!" Elle said. "It's going to blow you away! Well, I hope it doesn't blow you away so much that you can't concentrate, but that never happens to you—"

Chloe and Chessie arrived, giggling in their flirty miniskirts. "So, you're coming tonight, right?" Chessie said to Hunter.

Tonight? Where? Elle wondered.

"I'll be there," Hunter said. He went inside the gym. Chloe followed him.

Chessie turned and glanced at Elle. "I would have invited you," she said. "But dogs aren't allowed in my house. My mother's allergic."

"Oh," Elle said. "That's okay."

"I'm worried about you, Elle," Chessie said. "What if this nerd band stinks up the place tonight? Everyone knows it was all your idea. People might, I don't know, blame you. They might say you're a nerd-lover. Or other mean things. I just don't want to see you get hurt."

"Don't worry, Chessie," Elle said. "The band is going to be great. Have a good game!"

Elle was hurt that Chessie hadn't invited her to the party. How did Chessie even know she had a dog? And why would she have assumed that Elle would want to bring him? Of course, Elle *would* want to bring him, so, technically, somehow, Chessie was right.

Elle went inside and took her seat in the bustling gym. It still wasn't full, but, compared to the beginning of the season, attendance was great. Elle proudly noted a cluster of geeks in the right front bleachers, closest to where the brand-new band sat. Tonight was their basketball debut, and they'd invited some of their friends.

"Keep your fingers crossed," she said to Laurette as she took her customary seat. She held Underdog in her lap so everyone could be inspired by his Killer Bees spirit.

"You're taking a big risk, Elle," Laurette said. "Mixing nerds with jocks and cheerleaders—it just isn't done."

"Until now," Elle said. "Is Darren coming?"

Darren and Laurette had had a fantastic date the

weekend before. They'd gone to see an old movie, then driven around in Darren's beat-up old car and stopped at a diner for something to eat. They'd shared a milk shake. When he dropped her off, he had kissed her. Laurette was in heaven. But Darren still refused to take her to the Prom on philosophical grounds. It was the one thing spoiling Laurette's happiness.

"He said he'd pop his head in," Laurette said. "He wants to see what you've done with the band. But he can't take all the cheering and pep."

At the first time-out, the cheerleaders rushed on to the court. They started a new cheer while the band stumbled out after them and blurted out a corny old Tijuana Brass tune. They didn't usually perform in uniforms, so Sidney had arranged for everyone in the band to wear a *Star Trek* outfit. That was easy, since most of the musicians already owned one.

"Boo! You suck!" the crowd jeered, and not just from the opposing team.

Savannah scowled and marched over to Elle. Chessie followed her, hands on her hips. "Savannah is way pissed," Chessie said, even though Savannah was standing right there. "Get ready."

"Elle, have you lost it? What are those geeks doing interrupting our routines?" Savannah asked.

"Sorry, Savannah," Elle said. "They're supposed to wait until you're finished. It's their first time. They'll get better."

"And what's with the outfits?" Savannah said. "I don't like being associated with people who wear *Star Wars* costumes."

"Um, I think it's Star *Trek*, but—"

"Whatever. Get rid of them," Savannah said as she stormed away.

"You really blew it," Chessie said. "I'll try to calm her down." She chased after Savannah.

"Guess I've got more work to do," Elle said.

"Why don't you just get rid of the band?" Laurette asked.

"I can't," Elle said. "They're into it now. And look—they've brought a whole section full of spectators. I want the whole school to be behind this team. Not just the jocks. Not just the cool kids. Everyone. That's the energy we'll need to win."

"That and a miracle," Laurette said. "Beam me up, Scotty."

The band came out and tried a formation while they played "March of the Wooden Soldiers." They tried to make a giant *B,* but the bottom half collapsed and it ended up looking more like an *R,* which was unfortunate, since the opposing team was the Burbank Rockets. Meanwhile, the Rockets' band zipped on to the floor playing a Rolling Stones tune, while their cheerleaders danced.

"This is a washout," Laurette said.

"But at least the team is holding its own," Elle said.

The Bees eked out a win, 47–46. By the end, the band was too cowed to get out of their seats.

"How did we do, Elle?" Sidney asked. The band looked discouraged. They'd resisted becoming a marching band, but Elle had talked them into it, and now they were her responsibility.

"You'll be great once I totally revamp your look," Elle said. "And your sound. Let's meet after school on Monday. And for now, instead of *Star Trek* costumes, everyone wear a bright yellow shirt over black pants. You know, like bees. Okay?"

They dispersed. At least the rest of the crowd was happy. It was the third Beverly Hills win in a row. One more and they'd have a clear shot at the C-Conference championship. It was almost too much to hope for.

"Elle, tell me you're doing something about the band," Savannah said as she headed for the locker room. Chessie, as usual, was sticking to her like glue.

"I told her you tried your best, Elle," Chessie said. "But sometimes your best just isn't good enough."

"I'm fixing it, don't worry," Elle said.

"Good," Savannah said. "So I'll see you at Chessie's party?"

Chessie's face darkened. "I couldn't invite her, because of the dog."

"That's so stupid, Chessie," Savannah snapped. "She can drop the dog off at home if such a sweet little thing bothers you so much. Don't listen to her, Elle, come to the party."

"It's my house," Chessie protested, but Savannah waved her hand dismissively.

"I can't anyway," Elle said. "I've got something else to do." She didn't mention that the something else was stopping at a music store to buy new sheet music for the pathetic band.

"And a-one, and a-two," Elle counted as she coached the band in their new formation. "Remember, this comes after 'We've Got the Funk,' segueing into 'Flight of the Bumblebee.' Got it?"

The band rehearsed one of Elle's new formations. Part of the band made a *C*, which stood for Culver City, the following Friday's opponents. The rest of the players made a shape like a bee with a long stinger, which ran into the *C* and stung it. The *C* dissolved into a baby's face, with a wide-open mouth, while the band played "Crybaby." Then the whole band made a menacing skull and crossbones and played a tough rap song. They wore multicolored tissue-paper tops over their yellow Beverly Hills High T-shirts (Elle had them made herself) to help illustrate the different pictures. They could tear off each layer of color as needed, littering the floor with a festive confetti of ripped paper, which they would quickly clear away as they left.

Before the end of practice, Elle taught them one more tune. It was a new school fight song. A friend of Eva's was a songwriter, and Elle had asked him to whip up something catchy.

We are the Killer Bees! We'll bring you to your knees! Don't mess with Beverly Hills! We may look slick, but our freeze-glare kills! So bring it on, bring it, bring it! Do your worst, do it, do it! Can't touch us, can't muss us! We've got the style, we've got the power! Forever young, the mighty blue and gold! Even our grandparents don't look old! So call your lawyers, update your wills! We are mighty Beverly Hills!

♥   ♥   ♥

By the following Friday's game, the band was ready. They played rock, pop, and hip-hop songs that got the crowd moving, and their formations were so funny even the Culver City fans cheered. The stands were packed. Elle had printed out the words to the new school fight song and left a copy on every seat so the crowd could sing along. By the end of the night, the students were humming it. And, best of all, the Bees won again!

"That's it, ladies and gentlemen," the announcer said. "If the Beverly Hills Killer Bees win their next two games—and the Santa Monica Speedsters lose at least one more—the Bees are going to the championships!"

The crowd went crazy. The cheerleaders leaped, the basketball players grinned and high-fived, the band blared the school fight song, and the whole gymnasium, packed to the rafters, rocked, as hundreds of Beverly Hills students, from glams to geeks, sang along.

"Look what you did," Laurette said, almost as amazed as Elle. "You transformed this school. Just like you said you would." She turned and stared straight into Elle's eyes. "Are you a genie or something? Do you have magic powers? Were you sent here from another planet to save us from destruction?"

"*I* didn't do this," Elle said, her eyes on the prize, the victorious, glorious Hunter. "It's the power of love. Love makes everything it touches bloom!"

"That's one heck of a love you've got there," Laurette said.

"I know," Elle said.

Chapter 19

"SO, HAS Lisa LaRue decided anything yet?" John Fourier asked Elle.

"Who?" Elle asked.

Elle and Laurette and practically everybody from school were at a postgame party at Ryan's house, celebrating that night's victory. Even the band geeks came, and the basketball players told them how much they liked their skull-and-crossbones formation.

"You know, that casting agent," John said. "Isn't she a friend of your father's?"

"Oh, right. Lisa LaRue." Elle had almost forgotten about Zosia's little impersonation. "She doesn't talk business with me. Those casting decisions are usually top secret. But she did say she loves the way the Beverly players work together. And the comeback story has totally tugged at her heartstrings."

"It has been a great season," John said. He was tall—though not as tall as Hunter—and good-looking—ditto. And he was a nice guy, and the second-best player on the team. Elle liked him.

"I'll be so happy if we make it to the championships," he said. "And after that, it would be cool to have a cute girl to take to the Prom." He played with the zipper on his jacket.

At that moment, Elle spotted Hunter across the room. "Yes, the Prom," she sighed. "The perfect end to the perfect spring."

"I think so, too," John said. "I'm glad we agree."

Hunter smiled at Elle and motioned to her to come over. "I'll talk to you later, John," she said. What could Hunter want? She couldn't wait to find out.

She wove through the crowd. "I've got to talk to you, Elle," Hunter said. He remembered her name!

"Yes?" she said, tilting her chin in a way she hoped looked confident yet alluring. She'd seen Savannah do it a dozen times. *Ask me to the Prom*, she prayed. *Ask me to the Prom. . . .*

"Do you have a copy of *Hoosiers* at home?" Hunter asked. "I thought we could screen it for the team after practice next week. You know, to motivate us."

"Sure," Elle said. She tried to keep smiling even though she was disappointed. "I'll bring it to school on Monday. After all, I am assistant manager."

"Right," Hunter said. "You're the best, Elle."

The best? In what way? The best girl to take to the Prom?

"I mean it," Hunter said. "You're a great assistant manager."

Oh.

Chessie came by and took Hunter's hand. "Hunter, come on," she said. "You said we were going to dance. I put on your favorite song."

"I'm coming," Hunter said. He grinned at Elle and added, "Don't forget to bring the movie."

"I won't," Elle said. She watched Hunter and Chessie dance. Hunter moved on to dance with Jenna and Chloe, and then Chessie grabbed him back. But he was having a good time. And why wouldn't he? They were all gleaming, glittery, beautiful girls. Prom material. Elle wished he thought of *her* that way. Instead, he thought of her as the assistant manager.

♥　♥　♥

"I don't get it," Elle said. "Why doesn't Hunter like me? I've done everything I can—haven't I? I got rid of my braces and glasses, I'm wearing fabulous new clothes, my nails and my makeup are always perfect. I've helped him get close to his dream of playing on a championship basketball team before he graduates from high school. I've helped the entire school pull together and get behind his team. He's even thanked me for it. What else can I do?"

"You know what?" Bibi said. "I had a dream about you last night. One of those supervivid dreams you remember so well it feels real for hours after you wake up."

"You did? What happened?"

"Nothing much happened," Bibi said. "But I saw a girl in the dream, a girl who looked like you. She looked like a princess—she was wearing a beautiful gown, and beams of light radiated from her as if she were lit from inside. She wore a delicate, jeweled crown on her head, and she looked exactly like you—she *was* you—except for one thing."

"What?"

"She had long, silky, golden, sunny, blonde hair."

Elle was silent. She sat perfectly still. She could

see the image Bibi described as if the vision were standing in front of her under the heat lamps.

"Elle, that dream was a prophecy," Bibi said. "You know what I think it meant?"

Elle thought she knew, but she said, "What?"

"You need to go blonde. Highlights. It's your destiny."

"Do you think so?"

"I'm positive," Bibi said. "It wouldn't take much—your hair is basically dark blonde now. It would look totally natural on you."

"You're right," Elle said. "That's it. That's what I've been missing all this time. Blonde hair! Savannah has it. Chessie has it. Almost all of the cheerleaders are blonde. That must be why Hunter thinks I'm not his type—because he likes blondes."

"I wouldn't go that far," Bibi said. "Most boys aren't so rigid that they only like one color hair. But forget about Hunter for a second. Think about yourself. Your personality. You're bubbly, you're sweet, you're generous and sunny . . . You *are* a blonde at heart. Blonde hair would just be an expression of your true spirit."

Elle stared at herself in the mirror, trying to imagine her long, straight, mousy hair as a shiny veil of gold.

"It looked so amazing in the dream," Bibi said.

Elle trusted Bibi. She hadn't steered her wrong yet.

"Let's do it," Elle said. "Let's go blonde."

"Hooray!" Bibi leaped up and touched her toes, cheerleader style. "Right this way. This is going to change your life—you wait and see."

"Ta-da!" Elle walked into the house just before dinner. Eva and Wyatt were out on the patio having a predinner cocktail. Bernard was stirring the pitcher of drinks, and Zosia was serving them canapés.

Elle walked in, fresh from Pamperella, with her hair tucked into a newsboy cap. Her parents looked up.

"Elle, take off that silly hat," Eva said.

"All right." Elle cheerfully whipped the cap off her head. Piles of beautiful, golden hair tumbled down her back. Eva's jaw fell open. Everyone stared.

"Miss, you've changed your hair," Bernard said.

Recovering from the shock, Eva jumped up, knocking a plate of crackers with caviar to the stone floor. "Darling, you look lovely!" she cried. She threw her arms around Elle and kissed her repeatedly on the cheek.

"Mom, it's only highlights," Elle said, but she

knew the highlights looked good. Bibi had been right. Blonde hair suited her.

"Sweet little pussycat, you're a vision," Wyatt said.

Zosia kissed the tips of her fingers in a gesture of appreciation. "Your transformation is complete! You are a beauty!"

"Look at you!" Eva cried again. She stepped back to take her daughter in. "A real Beverly Hills girl. I can't believe it. Not so long ago you were shuffling around in those baggy old clothes—I thought I'd never get you to change. And now—" Tears sprang to her eyes. "It's a dream come true. And not a moment too soon. I was beginning to be afraid you'd taken after your father's side of the family."

Wyatt stiffened. "And what do you mean by that?"

"Darling, you know," Eva said. "Do I really have to say it? Aunt Gertrude?" Elle's aunt Gertrude was on the stocky side, and showed a complete indifference to fashion.

"If you're speaking of my sister Gertrude, I'll remind you that she was a very successful pro golfer in her day," Wyatt said.

"Oh, I know; I know," Eva said.

"Though even I will admit she's about as grace-ful as a walrus," Wyatt said.

"Dad came from his side of the family, too," Elle said. "And he's the most elegant man I know."

"Thank you, pussycat."

"You're right, of course," Eva said. "Otherwise I never would have married him. So at last you are growing up to be a girl people might recognize as our daughter. Let's celebrate! Bernard, break out the champagne. I'll start planning your debutante party."

"Mom, I don't need a deb party. And anyway, that's two years away."

"You can't send out the invitations too early," Eva said. "People in this town get booked up fast."

Elle knew her parents loved her, and she knew them well enough to realize that in spite of the way they phrased things, they were proud of her.

Elle heard a familiar tune as soon as she stepped onto the school grounds Monday morning. The school fight song. People were humming it, whistling it, even singing it out loud.

School spirit, Elle thought. Beverly Hills High is becoming a community at last.

There was another change, too. Elle, newly blonde, was whistled at, stared at, and asked out by three boys before she reached the front door.

I'll show everyone who's Promworthy, she thought.

"Elle? I've got to ask you something." John Fourier chased Elle down the hall.

She stopped. "Good morning," she said. She felt like a new person, but weirdly, this new person seemed more herself than the old person did. She wasn't that different—still the same old Elle— except for the energy and confidence that seemed to buzz through her, starting at the roots of her hair. That Bibi. When she was right she was right.

"I was wondering . . ." John began. He looked nervous. Elle marveled at this. A popular, handsome, senior boy was nervous about talking to her, the assistant manager of the basketball team. It was a strange, new experience.

"Would you go to the Prom with me?" John finished.

Elle gasped. She didn't know what to say. The Prom? This was huge.

Did John like her? Why hadn't she ever noticed before?

Going to Prom was one of her big goals. But she wanted to go with Hunter—and only with Hunter. What if he didn't ask her? She might not get to go at all. It would be fun to go with John . . . but if she said yes, that would rule Hunter out altogether. She'd have to accept that Hunter wasn't going to ask her. And she wasn't ready to do that yet.

"I'm sorry, John," she said. "I can't. I already have a date."

His face fell. "Who are you going with?"

"Um, I can't say," Elle said. She didn't want it to get back to Hunter that she was counting on him to ask her.

He gave her a funny look. "What about Lisa LaRue? Do you think she'd be willing to go to a high-school Prom?"

Elle laughed. Zosia at the Prom with John? It definitely wasn't her speed. "Sorry, John, but I think she's a little too old for that. Don't tell her I said that, though."

That day, Elle was asked to the Prom by two other seniors, but she turned them both down. They weren't Hunter. And he was the only one she wanted. True love wasn't true love unless you stuck with it and made sacrifices.

"I wish somebody would ask me to the Prom," Laurette said. "Mostly, I wish Darren would. But he never will, so I wish another boy would, just to show him how stupid he's being."

"I wish that, too," Elle said.

"All he cares about is his stupid band," Laurette said. "And being cool."

"He cares about you, too," Elle said.

"I'd like to see him prove it," Laurette said.

Chapter 20

"REBOUND!" *Clap, clap, clap!* "Rebound!" *Clap, clap, clap!*

You might think you broke our hearts. But now who's tearing who apart? The Bees are on the rebound! You can't stop us now! Feel our mighty sting! We'll knock you out. Ka-pow!

The cheerleaders neatly dismounted from an impressive flying pyramid as the Beverly Hills crowd hooted. Only Elle—and Savannah—noticed Chessie's tiny stumble at the end.

Another Friday night basketball game, another

great game for Beverly Hills. If they beat the Speedsters that night, they were going to next week's championship game! If they lost, the Speedsters would play the tough Chino Chargers.

Elle, Laurette, and Zosia sat surrounded by admiring boys. Sidney kept looking up at Elle from the right bleachers, where the band sat.

"Your new hair color is drawing them like flies, Your Blondness," Laurette teased.

"Elle, can I get you some popcorn?" one boy offered.

"No, thanks," Elle said.

Zosia leaned close and whispered, "No! Accept! A real coquette lets boys be her slaves. That's what they really want, deep down."

Elle blushed. "But I don't want a slave. I just want—"

Zosia put her finger to Elle's lips to shut her up. "Not so loud! Keep the other boys guessing!"

Zosia had volunteered to become Elle's flirting coach. She seemed to know everything.

The band came out and did a funny marching formation of a sports car crashing into a wall and exploding into flames, to the tune of "Wipe Out." The Beverly Hills crowd laughed and cheered appreciatively. The band had become like a musical comedy troupe—some students' favorite part of every game.

Elle gripped Laurette's hand. "Only three minutes left! And it's so close!" The score was 45–47, with the Speedsters up by two.

John passed the ball to Ryan, who dribbled down the court using Bernard's signature Bra Stuffer move and passed to Hunter. Hunter took a shot—two points! The score was tied! The gym roared.

There were two minutes left. Elle kept her eyes on her beloved Hunter. "You can do it," she murmured in a little prayer. "I know you can do it."

Santa Monica scored again. Then Hunter set up a shot for Aaron, who missed. Hunter got the rebound and scored two more points. The score was tied once again, with thirty seconds left!

"I can't stand it!" Zosia dug her red nails into Elle's arm.

With five seconds left, Hunter took a Hail Mary shot from half-court in a desperate attempt to win the game. The ball rolled around the rim . . . and bounced out. The crowd groaned.

"Oh, no," Laurette said. "They'll have to go into overtime."

But the referee blew his whistle. "Personal foul!"

he called, pointing in Santa Monica's direction. "Beverly Hills gets three penalty shots!"

The Beverly Hills fans screamed with excitement. The ref gave Hunter the ball. If he made just one of his three foul shots, the Bees would win. They'd go to the championships! If he missed, their season was over.

Hunter took his first shot. He missed. The Santa Monica fans waved flags and stamped their feet, trying to distract him. His second shot hit the rim and bounced out.

Elle closed her eyes. *Please make it, please make it. . . .* she thought.

Her eyes popped open. She had to watch. She couldn't miss Hunter's big moment. And she knew this would be a major one.

He bounced the ball twice. He had the cutest little line across his forehead when he concentrated. Then he shot the ball.

Swish! It went in! The clock ran out, and the buzzer blared. The Bees were going to the championships!

The Beverly Hills students poured on to the court, hugging and screaming and jumping up and down. The cheerleaders shouted, and the band played the fight song. Everyone sang along.

Savannah grabbed Elle and hugged her as they moshed through the crowd. "We're going to the championships!" she squealed. "Who would have believed it! It's because of you! You had faith! You made it happen!"

Elle was bowled over. Savannah was complimenting her—and hugging her! This wasn't ice-princess behavior.

She caught Hunter's eye. He was surrounded by admirers. He pointed his finger at her, then gave her a thumbs-up as he beamed with happiness. He was yelling something at her, but it was hard to hear over all the noise. She thought he was saying, "You're the one! You're the one!"

"What's he saying?" she shouted at Laurette. "I'm the one?" The one what? The one he wanted to take to the Prom?

"He's saying, 'We're number one,'" Chessie said, accidentally stepping on Savannah's foot.

"Chessie—Ow! Get off!" Savannah snapped.

"Sorry." Chessie turned red and melted away into the crowd.

"She's such a klutz," Savannah said. "I'm this close to kicking her off the squad. I would, except she's so good at doing chores for me. She can be useful, I'll give her that. Lousy cheerleader, though."

The ice princess was back. The thaw hadn't lasted long, but it had been nice.

The party that night was at Pacifico. Beverly Hills kids had taken over the place, but Elle had never been there before. It was dark and sleek, with long, glossy, black corridors leading from a large main dancing room into small, candlelit lounges.

Elle had gone home after the game to change. She now wore a red silk Chinese dress with a blue dragon embroidered on the back, and strappy gold sandals. Zosia had helped her do her makeup and hair, which was piled dramatically on top of her head with little wisps curling around her face. If a stranger had seen Elle only a few weeks earlier he would never have recognized her at Pacifico. The two Elles were from two different planets, the planet Schlub and the planet Glam. And Elle had to admit she liked the atmosphere on planet Glam a lot better.

She arrived at the party with Laurette and Darren, who was dressed in his usual rocker style, with ripped jeans and a vintage T-shirt, while Laurette wore a psychedelic sixties baby-doll dress with big white plastic earrings, go-go boots, and a wide hair band.

"Not to brag or anything, but we look fabulous," Laurette said as they strolled in to the party. It was already packed. The DJ was playing dance music, and the Beverly Hills kids had plenty to celebrate.

Chessie, in the same designer-jeans-and-sparkly-halter uniform that most of the cheerleaders wore, stopped Elle at the entrance. "You guys? Theme Night is Wednesday. I'm sorry—I must have forgotten to tell you."

"We're not here for Theme Night," Laurette said. "These are our clothes? This is called style?"

"Oh—right, I forgot," Chessie said. "This is your thing. I just thought I'd say something so you'd have time to go home and change if you wanted to, but . . . anyway, Elle, I have big news! I wanted to tell you because you've been such a sweet friend lately."

"Big news? What is it?" Elle asked.

"Brace yourself," Chessie said. "It's something we've all been hoping for for a while now. You're going to be so thrilled!"

"What?"

"It's about Hunter," Chessie said.

"Hunter!" Elle heart pounded. What about Hunter? Had Chessie heard him say something about the Prom?

"I wanted to tell you right away," Chessie said. "Hunter is going to ask me to the Prom tonight!"

"What?" The pounding of Elle's heart began to hurt. The music, the dancers, everything seemed to stop dead. Elle could hardly speak.

"I thought I should tell you before you hear it from someone else," Chessie said. "As a gesture of friendship. I think we should be closer. Confide in each other more."

"What?" Elle said again. It was all she could manage to say. She turned to Laurette for help.

"Chessie, you witch, how do you know this?" Laurette asked.

"I'm not talking to *you*, Laurette," Chessie said. "But if you must know, after the game, Hunter asked me if I was going to be here. He said I should be sure to find him, because he had something very important to ask me. What else could it be?"

The music roared in Elle's ears. She felt dizzy. Chessie was right—what else could it be? He must want to ask her to the Prom. Her, and not Elle. After all her hard work, after taking the basketball team so far and the rest of the school along with it, how could this part of Elle's dream not come true? It was the most important part! It was the key to the whole dream.

"Elle, aren't you thrilled?" Chessie said. "Where's my hug?"

Elle hugged her. "I'm really happy for you, Chessie," she said. And she tried to be. It was wonderful for Chessie. Elle wanted her to be happy. If only it didn't mean taking Hunter away!

All this time, Darren had been watching the crowd with half an ear on the girls' conversation. "Um, this sounds like the kind of thing I don't need to be involved in," he said. "Anybody want a drink?"

Laurette asked him for a cranberry-and-soda, and he went to the bar. Just mentioning the Prom seemed to drive him away.

"There he is!" Chessie pointed out a khaki-covered knee just visible in one of the cozy lounges. It was Hunter, all right. "Wish me luck! Not that I need it. Elle, I think John Fourier is going to ask you to the Prom. Then we can go as a foursome!"

"He already asked me," Elle said.

"Great!" Chessie said.

"I turned him down," Elle said.

"What? Why?" Chessie made a fake frowny face. "Oh, I get it—you want to go with Ryan!"

"Laurette and I aren't going," Elle said. "We've got something else to do."

"What could be better than going to the Senior

Prom?" Chessie asked. "Well, I guess there's always next year. Bye!" She hurried into the lounge. Hunter, surrounded by girls, as usual, and a few of his teammates, smiled at her.

"I can't believe he's going to ask her," Elle said. "I thought it was my destiny to go with him. I really did. Look how well everything else has turned out. But if I can't go to the Prom with Hunter, what's the point?"

"She's full of it," Laurette said. "Don't let her get to you. She could have made that whole story up just to psych you out." She paused before continuing. "Elle, Chessie is not your friend. Don't you get it yet? She doesn't care about you. She only cares about herself."

In her memory, Elle replayed her interactions with Chessie over the last few months. She saw herself feeling fine, then talking to Chessie, then drooping, her spirits wilting. It was true, Chessie made her feel bad.

"You're right, Laurette," Elle said. "She's not nice. And I can't stand the thought of Hunter going to Prom with a girl who's not nice. Especially if she's not me. He deserves better than that!"

"Look—she's talking to him!" Laurette said. "She's probably trying some sneaky trick to get him to ask her to Prom. She's going after your guy, Elle! Do something! Stop her!"

Laurette gave Elle a little push.

That was all Elle needed. Across the room she saw Savannah slow-dancing with her lacrosse hunk, Bryce. Savannah always got her man.

Savannah will be my inspiration, Elle thought. She'd never let someone like Chessie steal her guy.

Elle marched over to the circle of admirers surrounding Chessie and Hunter.

Be like Savannah, she told herself. What would Savannah do?

Chessie was smiling up at Hunter, chattering away, not letting him get a word in edgewise, and flirtatiously twirling a lock of blonde hair around her finger. "I guess, after Savannah, I'm the star cheerleader," Chessie was saying. "I'm the one who totally revamped the squad. I wrote all those new cheers, and taught everybody new moves. I could see that the old stuff we were doing was lame. Savannah's grateful to me. She told me so. She said I saved the squad." She paused to walk her fingers up Hunter's shirt, from one button to the next. "I think that had just a *little* effect on the basketball team, don't you? Amping up school spirit? Helping you guys win?"

Elle was fuming. How dare she? How dare Chessie stand there and take credit for all Elle's hard work?

What would Savannah have done? Elle didn't even have to think about it. She'd seen it happen so many times before that it kicked in like a reflex. Savannah would have put Chessie in her place.

"Chessie, stop teasing Hunter," Elle said. "Everyone knows you're just a placeholder. You've got two left feet. Savannah told you that if you tried to do anything more than a few claps and stomps, she'd kick you off the squad."

Chessie's mouth fell open.

"I'm just telling the truth," Elle said. "She's a total klutz," she said to Hunter. "Ask Chloe, or anyone on the squad."

Chessie went pale. Then she turned and ran away. Elle suddenly felt terrible—worse than she had ever felt after one of Chessie's double-edged comments.

What have I done? she thought.

"That was harsh," Hunter said. "I didn't think you were that kind of girl, Elle."

"I—I didn't mean to hurt her feelings," Elle said. "But she was lying about cheerleading, and—"

"And you thought you'd set the record straight

for her, huh?" Hunter said. "That little put-down was a classic Savannah move. Maybe you've been spending a little too much time with her. I should have gotten a hint when you started wearing those hot clothes and went blonde. Listen, Elle—whatever you do, don't turn into Savannah. Maybe she didn't tell you this, but I dumped her, and I dumped her for a reason—she's mean and selfish. It took me a while to figure it out, but I finally learned my lesson, the hard way. And I don't care how pretty or cool a girl is. If she's not nice, she's history."

Elle wanted to hide her face and never show it again. She felt so low. Chewed out by Hunter! She hardly ever got close to him, and when she finally did, what did she do? Showed him her worst side! And hurt Chessie in the bargain.

"I—I'm sorry," Elle said. "I've got to go."

She ran straight out of the club.

Chapter 21

"WHY DID you file my nails so pointy?" Elle asked at her regular appointment with Bibi that weekend. "Are they supposed to be claws? Are you trying to tell me something?"

"Relax, Elle," Bibi said. "I just thought I'd try out a new shape. Why are you so edgy today?"

"Everything has fallen apart," Elle confessed. "Bibi, am I becoming mean? Am I turning into a Savannah—in a bad way?"

"Mean? What are you talking about?"

"I wanted to go to Prom with Hunter so badly," Elle said. "But Chessie told me he was going to ask *her*. So when I saw her talking to him, I said something mean about her, right in front of him.

To embarrass her. So he wouldn't like her better than me."

"That is kind of mean," Bibi said. "Why did you do that? It doesn't sound like you at all."

"I was trying to do what Savannah would have done," Elle said. "Savannah always gets her man."

"Maybe so," Bibi said. "But you don't have to be like Savannah to get what you want. You've got your own way of doing things that works just fine. Look how far you've come already, in just a few weeks! You've done more than Savannah's done in a lifetime, I bet. And you did it all without being mean to anybody."

Elle felt better hearing Bibi's words. She didn't want to be mean—it didn't suit her. And she didn't have to! Things would work out. Maybe not with Hunter, but in every other way. She didn't need to go to Prom. Laurette wasn't going. They could have fun doing something else together. And as Chessie had said, there was always next year.

"How do you always know just the right thing to say, Bibi?"

"Practice," Bibi said.

"Are they shooting a movie or something?" Laurette asked as they drove to school on Monday morning.

"Everything looks different. What are all those flags for?"

The streets of Beverly Hills had been transformed by Killer Bees fever. Houses flew blue-and-gold flags and "Go, Bees!" banners. Cars decorated with blue-and-yellow crepe paper cruised through the streets, honking their horns. The whole neighborhood was excited about the championship game. It was very un–Beverly Hills.

"It does look like a movie set," Elle said. "Like some small town in the Midwest where basketball is everything."

"Yeah, not like a place where the school fight song mentions lawyers and plastic surgery," Laurette said.

They parked in the school lot and walked up to the main entrance. Elle pushed open the door. "Wow," she gasped.

"It's like Mardi Gras in May," Laurette said.

The hallway was covered with decorations. A huge gold banner was draped across the entrance. On it, in blue letters, were written the words "GO, BEES!" There were blue-and-gold fliers and posters and pictures of killer bees everywhere. A lot of the students were wearing blue-and-gold clothes or Beverly Hills High T-shirts and caps.

And the halls were buzzing with excited talk about the big game on Friday. The basketball championships! Everyone was excited. People hummed the school fight song as they walked to their classes.

"Are we in the right school?" Laurette asked.

"This is amazing," Elle said. "Look at all this school spirit!"

A clutch of guys and girls wore T-shirts that said, *I'm with the band* on the front and *BHH Marching Band* on the back.

"The band has groupies now," Laurette said. "Bet those geeks are glad they let you talk them into that."

"I hope so," Elle said. "I'll talk to you later. I've got to apologize to Chessie. And then I've got to find Hunter and straighten things out. I don't want him to think I'm evil, even if he doesn't want to take me to the Prom."

"Good luck convincing him Chessie's not a klutz," Laurette said. "That's going to take some talking."

"Laurette! No more meanness," Elle said.

"What do you want?" Chessie snapped. Elle found her in the girls' bathroom, locked in a stall. She recognized Chessie's size-ten Marc Jacobs sandals under the stall door.

"Chessie, let me in," Elle said.

Chessie opened the door. "I'll come out," she said. "I'm sick of this stupid stall anyway." She kicked open the door and walked out, her face red and tearstained. She walked to the sink and splashed water on her face.

"I spent the whole weekend crying," Chessie said. "I can't stop!"

"Chessie, I'm really sorry," Elle said. "I don't know what got into me. Actually, I do know, but it wasn't good."

"I thought you were my friend," Chessie said. "I'm always nice to you. Why would you turn on me like that in front of Hunter? Right when he was about to ask me to Prom?"

"I guess I was jealous," Elle said.

"And to *lie* like that," Chessie said. "Saying I'm clumsy! When anybody with eyes can see that I'm not!"

"I never should have said those things," Elle said. "Please forgive me, Chessie. I'll tell Hunter that it wasn't true, and how important you are to the squad. I know he'll believe me, and everything will be okay."

Chessie dried her face. She looked a little better now. "Do you promise?"

"I swear," Elle said. "Pinkie-swear." She stuck out her pinkie. Chessie hooked her pinkie over it, and they shook on it.

"You'll see," Elle said. "Everything will work out for the best."

"It'd better, Elle," Chessie said. "Or I won't be nice to you anymore."

"Rachel! How could you screw up like that?" The bathroom door burst open, and Savannah and Rachel stormed in. Rachel looked on the verge of tears.

"I'm sorry!" she wailed. "How was I supposed to know that DJ Clownface only did kiddie parties?"

"I think the name might have tipped you off," Savannah said.

"I thought it was ironic," Rachel said.

"What's the matter?" Elle asked.

"Rachel hired a kiddie DJ to do the music for the Prom," Savannah said. "We went to check him out and ended up at a kindergarten graduation party. He's terrible!"

"But we can't get anyone else," Rachel said. "The Prom is only two weeks away. All the good DJs are already booked."

Elle got that tingly feeling in her scalp that meant

that an idea was forming. "Don't worry, girls," she said. "I think I can solve your problem."

"How?" Chessie asked.

"Yeah, how?" Rachel looked skeptical.

"Trust me," Elle said.

"Why should we?" Rachel said. "You're just a sophomore."

"You know what?" Savannah said. "I've gotten to know this girl. And if she says to trust her, you can."

"Thanks, Savannah!" The compliment made Elle feel warm. Now all she had to do was prove Savannah right.

Elle ran into Darren in the hallway and watched his whole face lit up when he heard her proposal. His band was going to have a gig! And not only that, Elle smiled to herself as she walked to her next class, her best friend was going to have a date for the Senior Prom.

She didn't really have time to celebrate her victory, though. First she had to keep her promise to Chessie.

Elle found Hunter in the gym at lunchtime, practicing foul shots. She hated to interrupt him, but this was important.

"Hunter? Can I talk to you for a minute?"

"Sure." He took one more shot, then quit.

"I'm sorry about the other night," she said. "I didn't mean to put Chessie down. I apologized to her. But I wanted to make sure you knew that the things I said about her aren't true. She's a very valuable member of the cheerleading squad." Elle paused, trying to come up with a way in which Chessie contributed. It took some thinking. "She—she's a big help to Savannah, always picking up after the other girls and doing as she's told. And her voice is louder than anybody's! The squad would be terrible without her."

"Thanks for telling me that, Elle," Hunter said. "I knew you weren't really a Savannah or Chessie type. And I'm glad." He turned around and took another shot. The ball went in.

"Are you nervous about the championships?" Elle asked.

"No," Hunter said. "You know why? Because I've already gotten what I wanted. All I wanted was a good season, a good team, and some psyched fans. And somehow, like magic, it has all happened." He smiled at her. "Just shows what some people are capable of, when they put their minds to it."

The bell rang; it was time for them to get to class. But Elle could hardly concentrate on school. She felt the warmth of Hunter's smile on her face for the rest of the day.

Chapter 22

"COME ON, Ryan, pass to Hunter!" Elle shouted.

"Run the Fred at them!" Bernard yelled. "Fred!"

Their voices were lost among the screams of a huge crowd of cheering fans. Ryan took a shot from far outside the zone and missed by a mile. The Beverly Hills fans groaned. It was the fourth quarter, and the score was 51–44, Chino.

"We didn't come all this way just to lose," Laurette said. "Did we?"

The C-Conference championships had arrived at last. Beverly Hills High fans crammed into the gym at Chino High School, whose team had won the right to play at home, since it had the stronger record. Elle sat smushed on the crowded Beverly

Hills bleachers with Bernard, Zosia, Laurette, and Darren. Darren gripped Laurette's hand and kept his eyes glued to the court, as into the game as anybody. The whole school had been obsessed with basketball all week long, and this was the moment they'd been waiting for.

"Pass it!" Darren shouted as Aaron dribbled straight down the court. "Pass to Hunter!"

"This is the perfect setup for a Wedgie," Bernard said. "Aaron, pull a Wedgie!"

Instead, Aaron dribbled right into a Chino Charger and fouled him. The Bees fans groaned again. This was terrible.

"Bernard, what are they doing wrong?" Elle asked.

"They're nervous," Bernard said. "They're taking wild shots. And they're forgetting all their teamwork. They can't beat these Chino boys without teamwork. Look how tall the Chargers are."

It was true. The Chino boys were all huge. They towered over the Bees. But the Bees could use that to their advantage if they'd only remember the plays they'd been taught. If they'd only remember to work as a team.

"Maybe this will help," Elle said. She scrambled down the bleachers to where the cheerleaders and the band were sitting, discouraged.

"Sing the school fight song," Elle shouted at them. "All of you—the cheerleaders, the band—get the crowd into it. Let's all sing the school song together."

She returned to her seat. Coach Robinson called a time-out. The band and the cheerleaders flooded the court. The band struck up the melody, and the cheerleaders began to sing. Savannah waved at the crowd, encouraging them to join in.

We are the Killer Bees! We'll bring you to your knees! Don't mess with Beverly Hills! We may look slick, but our freeze-glare kills! So bring it on, bring it, bring it! Do your worst, do it, do it. Can't touch us, can't muss us! We've got the style, we've got the power! Forever young, the mighty blue and gold! Even our grandparents don't look old! So call your lawyers, update your wills! We are mighty Beverly Hills! Go, Bees!

The whole Beverly Hills crowd sang their hearts out, as if this were their national anthem. The boys on the team looked up at the crowd singing for them, touched. "Remember, we're a team!" Hunter shouted, so clearly that Elle could hear him all the way up in the bleachers. "Let's get it together. No more wild shots. Stick with the plays that got us here. No hotdog moves! Let's go!"

The ref blew his whistle, and the game resumed. The Bees pulled off a perfect Towel Snapper. Two points! The crowd cheered. The score was 52–46. They were only three baskets away from winning!

Chino scored; then Beverly Hills scored. Beverly Hills scored again, and Aaron was fouled by a Charger. His two foul shots went in. It was now 54–52, with two minutes left. They had to score three points to win—and they had to keep the Chargers from scoring, too.

Elle clung to Laurette, as terrified as if she had been watching a gory horror movie. "I can't take it! I can't take it!" she cried.

"Neither can I," Laurette said. "Especially since you're cutting off all the circulation in my arm."

"Sorry, but it can't be helped," Elle said.

The Chargers had the ball. They drove down the court and took a shot, but Hunter leaped up and snatched the ball out of midair. The crowd screamed. Thirty seconds to go! Hunter passed to John, who passed to Aaron, who passed back to

John, who passed to Hunter, who was just inside the half-court line. Time was running out. Hunter aimed and threw the ball as hard as he could at the basket.

The ball seemed to float through the air in slow motion. Elle held her breath. It bounced into the rim and rolled around, and around, and around . . . and sank through the net.

Three points! The Bees had won!

"We won! We won the championship!" The Beverly Hills stands were a riot of hugging and shouting and happy shrieks. Elle hugged everyone she could reach. She wanted to hug the whole world! But most of all, she wanted to hug Hunter.

Hunter's teammates piled on top of him as the fans flooded the court. When Hunter finally got out from under the pileup, the referee presented him with the Most Valuable Player trophy as well as the team's championship trophy. Hunter posed with the team, one trophy in each arm, as flashbulbs popped like shooting stars around them. The referee gave him a microphone, and everyone called for a speech.

"I want to thank everyone at Beverly Hills for giving the team such solid support," Hunter said. "Most of all, I'd like to thank the one person who pulled the school together to make this all happen—Elle Woods."

Elle gasped. Laurette pushed her through the crowd toward Hunter. He put his arm around her, kissed her on the cheek, and said, "Elle, you're more than assistant manager. You're part of the team."

The crowd cheered and clapped for Elle, for the team, for everyone. Elle bit her lip, trying not to cry. This was the most amazing moment of her life.

Elle sat on the bus, waiting for the team to finish changing. Everyone else had gone ahead to the victory party at Savannah's house, but as assistant manager, Elle thought she should ride back to Beverly Hills with the team. The bus driver paced outside, talking on the phone. Elle sat with her thoughts, happily reliving every moment of this winning season. She remembered that first rally, when Hunter had pleaded with the school for support, only weeks earlier. Everything was so different now. The team had gone from hopeless losers to champions. The every-kid-for-himself vibe of the school had been replaced by an all-together-now sense of belonging. And Elle herself—she could admit it, she knew it was true—had changed from a shy, mousy introvert to one of the prettiest and most popular girls at school.

Love did this, she thought. Love is so powerful it transformed a whole town and school! It brought me everything, except for the one thing I wanted most—Hunter.

She heard a footstep and looked up, expecting to see the bus driver. But it was Hunter, freshly showered and dressed in clean clothes, clutching a gym bag and his MVP trophy.

"Elle," he said. "I'm glad you're here."

He walked to the back of the bus, where she was sitting, and sat next to her.

"This is thanks to you," he said, pressing the trophy into her hands. "You should have it. My dream came true, and it's all because of your hard work."

Elle pushed the trophy back. "I can't take that. You totally earned it. You worked hard, too, you know. You're the one who scored those baskets."

"Please," he insisted. "Take it. You were the most valuable part of this team. I mean it."

He set the trophy in her lap and refused to let her give it back. "Well," she said. "I'll let it rest here until we get off the bus."

They sat in silence for a minute. Hunter's face was lit by a streetlamp outside the bus. He looked beautiful. Elle wished she had the nerve to kiss him. But he wouldn't want that. He liked Chessie.

"So, the Prom is next week," Hunter said.

"I know," Elle said.

"Are you going?"

"No," Elle said. "You should ask Chessie soon. I know she'll say yes. I'm sorry I interrupted you when you tried to ask her."

"What? Ask Chessie?" Hunter said. "I was never going to ask her to the Prom."

"But she told me—"

"I wanted to ask her if she thought my little sister could make the cheerleading squad next year. She's starting ninth grade in the fall, and she thinks these girls are cool."

"That's what you were going to ask her?" Elle said. "When I interrupted you at Pacifico?"

"Uh-huh." Hunter leaned close to Elle. She could smell the soap on his skin. "There's only one girl I want to ask to Prom. She's the queen of the school, and the prettiest little blonde I've ever seen." He kissed her, right on the lips. Elle closed her eyes. Her first kiss ever.

Her lips tingled. She forgot to breathe. Hunter sat up and looked into her eyes.

"So, what do you say?" he asked.

"About what?" The kiss had turned Elle's brain to mush.

Hunter laughed. "The Prom. Did you forget already?"

"Oh—were you talking about me just now?" Elle asked. "Queen of the school? I wasn't sure. I don't usually think of myself as royalty."

"Well, you should," Hunter said. "Will you be my date?"

"Yes!" Elle said.

They kissed again. How could she say no to fate?

Chapter 23

"ELLE! IS that my little pink pussycat?" Wyatt said. "Bernard, get me an oxygen tank. My little girl has taken my breath away!"

Elle stood at the top of the stairs, all dressed and ready for Prom. She had a fresh Bibi manicure, and Zosia had helped with her hair and makeup. Her mother had helped her pick out the perfect dress and shoes. No more mouse. She looked like a princess.

"It's a dream come true," Eva said. "Oh, Elle, this is how I always pictured you! Your shiny blonde hair in an updo, a chic pink Prada gown, stiletto heels . . ." She began to tear up.

"Careful, Mrs. Woods," Zosia warned. "Your eye job!" Eva had recently had her eye lift touched up.

"Oh, I know I shouldn't cry, but I can't help it!" Eva carefully dabbed at her eyes. Wyatt put his arm around her, toasting Elle with a martini he held in his other hand.

Elle started down the stairs, leading Underdog on a rhinestone leash. He wore a little black-and-white sweater Elle had made to look like a doggy tuxedo. The doorbell rang.

"I'll get it!" Zosia said. She opened the door. There stood Hunter, looking dashing in his Prada tux, worn chicly without a tie.

"Lisa LaRue!" Hunter said. "What are you doing here?"

Whoops. Elle had forgotten all about that little charade.

"And Coach Bernard," Hunter said. "What's going on?"

Elle stepped forward and said, "I'll explain in the limo."

Hunter smiled. "Wow, you look unbelievable."

"Doesn't she?" Wyatt said. "You two have a wonderful time."

Hunter offered Elle his arm, and Underdog trotted beside her.

"We will!" she said.

♥   ♥   ♥

"I'm so sad Laurette couldn't come tonight," Chessie said, tracing a pretend tear down her cheek. "Frowny face!"

John Fourier had asked Chessie to the Prom, which had helped her recover, just slightly, from losing Hunter to Elle. Elle and Chessie stood in front of the stage, watching the band set up, while John and Hunter went to get drinks.

"Laurette made her choice," Chessie said. "She had to like some dorky guy in a leather jacket who thinks he's too cool for the Prom. As if."

"What are you talking about?" Elle said. "Laurette's here."

"She is? How? Did she find another date?"

"No," Elle said. "Look." She nodded toward the band on the stage. Sprayed on the bass drum were the words WARP FACTOR 5. Darren stood behind the microphone, tuning his guitar. Laurette walked out from backstage, gave him a good-luck kiss, then spotted Elle and hurried over.

"You look great!" Elle said. Laurette was wearing a blue sequined mermaid dress with a big blue flower in her hair.

"So do you!" Laurette said. "I can't believe it! We're at the Senior Prom! Both of us. What are the odds?"

"I don't get it," Chessie said. "What happened?"

"Darren decided to come to the Prom after all," Elle said.

"Yeah, the committee needed a band, and Elle suggested the Factor," Laurette said. "Darren couldn't turn down his first gig!"

Hunter and John returned with the drinks. Soon the band started playing. Hunter took Elle by the hand and led her to the dance floor.

Elle stared up at the canopy overhead; there was a scattering of fake stars. The Prom committee had turned the hotel ballroom into a dreamy, romantic place. The theme of the dance was written in stars on the wall: DREAMS COME TRUE.

Elle looked at Hunter, who pulled her close.

Dreams do come true, Elle said to herself as she looked around at the scene. Then she gazed into Hunter's eyes. And I'm living proof, she thought.

"You know, Elle," Hunter said, "you've changed a lot since I first noticed you."

"I know," Elle said. And she liked it that way. No more mouse. She was blonde at heart. And she'd never go back.